Sneaking Suspicions

Carolyn Coman

Sneaking Suspicions

DRAWINGS BY
Rob Shepperson

Alameda Free Library
1550 Oak Street
Alameda, CA 94501

FRONT STREET
Asheville, North Carolina

ACKNOWLEDGMENTS

Captain Matt Johnson was the perfect tour guide through the Everglades, a gold mine of information that he shared in a helpful and easygoing way, answering my questions while I was there and after I got back home, too. Any facts I got straight are probably due to him, and all the crooked ones are my own doing.—C.C.

Text copyright © 2007 by Carolyn Coman
Illustrations copyright © 2007 by Rob Shepperson
All rights reserved
Printed in China
Designed by Helen Robinson
First edition

LIBRARY OF CONGRESS CATALOGING-IN-PUBLICATION DATA
Coman, Carolyn.
Sneaking suspicions / Carolyn Coman ; pictures by Rob Shepperson.—1st ed.
p. cm.
Summary: Ivy and Ray go on vacation to the Florida Everglades with their parents in
order to find their only living relative, a distant cousin who, according to their
great-grandfather's memoirs, absconded with a valuable, if unspecified, item.
ISBN 978-1-59078-491-4 (hardcover : alk. paper)
[1. Brothers and sisters—Fiction. 2. Family—Fiction. 3. Vacations—Fiction.
4. Swindlers and swindling—Fiction. 5. Everglades (Fla.)—Fiction.
6. Florida—Fiction. 7. Humorous stories.] I. Shepperson, Rob, ill. II. Title.
PZ7.C729Sne 2007
[Fic]—dc22   2006101610

FRONT STREET
An Imprint of Boyds Mills Press, Inc.
815 Church Street
Honesdale, Pennsylvania 18431

Sneaking Suspicions

Contents

A FORCE TO BE RECKONED WITH

Ivy Fitts sat tall and straight, a model of attention for the last minutes of the last morning of the last day of school. The stack of report cards, a paper tower, rose from Ms. Meanes's desk. Ivy stared at that tower and endowed herself with laser-beam eyes in an attempt to penetrate the envelope marked with her name. She especially wanted to X-ray the columns that ran along-

side the grades, the ones headed *Conduct* and *Effort*. There she visualized a perfect row of check marks, precise and approving. What she feared was an accompanying row of minuses, those miserly little dashes diminishing the glory of her checks one by one. Banish the thought! For each minus Ivy imagined, she quickly inserted a mental crossbar, and—*bingo!*—a bouquet of check-pluses bloomed inside her head. A few simple lines could change everything.

Now Ivy turned her interior attention to the back of her report card—the space where Ms. Meanes wrote what she called her narrative. Ivy could picture her teacher's lovely, looping cursive, and she willed Ms. Meanes's description of her to contain words like *hands-down winner* and *top dog* and *blistering genius*. For the first time in her life Ivy had gone to the same school for the entire year, and she figured that alone merited commendation.

Bit by bit a swelling hope rose inside her as she waited to receive her report card—a sneaking suspicion that she just might have a shot at Student of the Year. Spelling wasn't everything; it didn't even count, as far as Ivy was concerned. And most of the worst things she'd been caught red-handed doing had

happened at the beginning of the year, a distant memory. Ms. Meanes didn't seem the type to hold a grudge. Why *shouldn't* she be Student of the Year? Ivy asked herself. She imagined a certificate, a plaque, a trophy. She pictured herself walking up to receive the award, and music swelled in the background, a rousing tune, trumpets. Drums. It occurred to her suddenly that perhaps there would be a cash prize as well. The thought sat her up an extra inch.

Ms. Meanes plucked the envelope from the top of the stack and called the first name. "Archibald Ames."

Ivy's heart commenced hammering. Straight-A Archie. He bounded up to the desk. So what that he was a good speller, last man standing in every bee.

"Felicia Buttersworth."

Ivy could never look at Felicia without envying her ability to touch her tongue to her nose.

"Hector Bonovitch."

Ivy counted on her fingers how many more kids would be called—those with last names beginning with *C* and *D* and *E*—until, finally, it would be *F* for Fitts, her turn. That was when things would *really* begin for Ivy. She thought about her brother, Ray, down the hall, and wondered if he had been called yet. Tests and grades and being forced to walk up to the teacher's desk in front of everyone else gave him a stomachache.

"Zena Cadafy."

Ivy let the music in her head play in the background, accompaniment to her thoughts of straight A's, Student of the Year, the start of summer, the trip her family would be taking. A Fitts family meeting was scheduled for that night to decide where they would go and what they would do. For weeks, Ivy and Ray had been adding to their list of desirable destinations.

"Octavio Diaz."

Ivy felt strongly that her family was overdue in the vacation department. Last summer their plans had been foiled when her parents, Dan and Carol, got sent to prison and Ivy and Ray ended up living with Marietta and Lionel. This year had been better because Dan and Carol were out of prison and they were all back together in Marietta and Lionel's big house, living in what Dan called the lap of luxury. They even had a chauffeur—Veddy—and drove around in a limousine. All of this thanks to the fortune Ray and Ivy had inherited from their great-grandfather Blackstone Mouton.

"Manny Dickerson."

Manny shuffled up. He was the biggest troublemaker in the class, hands down. Ivy imagined the Conduct and Effort columns on *his* report card and consoled herself with the thought that hers had to be better. But Manny was all smiles as he collected his envelope from Ms. Meanes, and he gave Ivy two thumbs up on his return.

Ivy nodded and went back to thinking about vacation. She and Ray had spun the globe in the library to find good places, dragging their fingers across the continents and calling out where they were when the earth stopped spinning. Malaysia, Mexico, the USSR. Ivy especially liked islands, and squiggles of land that jutted out from all the others, places that were at the edge. She also liked places with good names: Katmandu, Iceland, Singapore.

Dan had told them that the globe was ancient

history. "Hate to break it to you," he said, "but some of those places don't exist anymore."

"Where'd they go?" Ray asked.

"Nowhere," Dan said. "But they go by different names now."

"Oh." Going by different names was no big deal to Ray and Ivy. They even knew the word for it: *alias.* So they kept right on spinning the ancient-history globe and calling out names. If they landed in the ocean they got to go again.

"Kieisha Emory."

Kieisha was OK. She was shy, the way Ray was. She had long eyelashes that looked as if they curled out from the curve of her round cheeks because she was so often looking down.

"Alice Evans." Evans: the final *E.*

The music swelled.

"Ivy Fitts."

How she loved hearing her name called out—the Ivy *and* the Fitts of it, the sound and soundness of both of them. And she especially liked her name when paired with applause. Ivy marched to the front of the class and reached out her hand for the envelope. But Ms. Meanes extended her other hand first, the empty one, for Ivy to shake. The movie that was playing in Ivy's head—in which Ivy was standing in front of her cheering classmates, about to receive a prizewinning report card—momentarily stopped, and then she brought her hand over to Ms. Meanes for a quick, strong shake, and the movie continued.

"Congratulations, Ivy," Ms. Meanes said, her smile wide, her lipstick red. She finally delivered the envelope.

Ivy pivoted and began her walk back to her desk, past rows of clapping classmates. Chester Fitzgerald had already been called and was on his way up, but Ivy felt certain the continuing applause was for her. She carried her envelope like a platter, on the palms of both hands.

Settled at her desk, she ached to bend back the little silver clasp and inch out the report card and take a peek. But they had been warned: no looking until all the cards had been distributed and Student of the Year announced. She spread her hands over her envelope, as if she might divine through her fingertips the good news that was spelled out within.

Ms. Meanes carried on, calling name after name;

Ivy watched the black needle on the clock pulse forward around the seconds of the school day—and year—that remained.

Finally Ms. Meanes lifted the last envelope from her desk and handed it to Ila Zacker. Generally Ivy found Ila sluggish, but at that moment she felt a little sorry for him, always last simply because *Zacker* began with a Z. Everyone clapped, Ila claimed his card and returned to his seat, and the whole class looked to Ms. Meanes, expectant.

Her red lipstick glowed. Her white teeth shone. She clapped her hands together and took a deep breath. "Student of the Year goes to ..." Ivy was sure Ms. Meanes looked directly at her for one poignant second. "Archibald Ames."

Ivy's ears burned as if they had been slapped. Clapping erupted all around her. The movie inside her head stopped playing entirely. Archie shot up to the desk and shook Ms. Meanes's hand. She spun him out to face front and patted him on the back and gave him a certificate with a gold stamp and a ribbon on it—a red ribbon, its ends notched in upside-down V's. He returned to his desk, the final bell exploded, and school was out.

It was over like that—in a flash—and though it had not gone as Ivy had hoped or dreamed, she was already scrambling to recover, working hard and fast to see her way around it. Who needed Student of the Year? Summer vacation had begun! How many times had Dan told her to keep her eyes on the prize? And as for the prize—she was sure there was an explanation for why she hadn't won. All she had to do was think it up. Maybe she had been first choice for the prize, but Ms. Meanes felt sorry for Archie because he had *bald* in his name. Maybe Archie had *bribed* Ms. Meanes. Maybe—though it was a ridiculous thought—spelling *did* matter.

As classmates sprang up around her and headed for the door, Ivy stayed seated and opened the clasp on her envelope. She pulled out the card and scanned the front. Her grades—except for spelling—were fine, even if there weren't as many pluses as there might have been. Effort was more or less OK, too. But the Conduct column was riddled with those lonely little dashes. Ivy glared at Ms. Meanes through narrow eyes, resented her for remembering past transgressions. Then she flipped the card over to read Ms. Meanes's narrative.

Ivy's imagination is a force to be reckoned with—a land

of wild conjecture and bubbling theories, some of them quite original. Despite a number of unfortunate lapses in judgment and behavior over the course of the year, Ivy was a wonderful source of energy in our class. If we can keep her on the straight and narrow, I have no doubt Ivy will make her mark on the world.

Ivy's clenched heart softened as she read—and immediately reread—those final, beautiful words: *make her mark on the world.* She liked *quite original,* too. And *a force to be reckoned with* had a pleasing ring to it. The pinch and sting of Archie stealing the prize from her faded a bit as she savored the good words of the narrative. She read it over one more time—just the parts she liked—and then slid the card back into the envelope. She stood up, head held high, relieved, recovered, ready to go.

Ray was waiting for her by her locker, springy with excitement that school was finally done. His folded-up report card stuck out from his back pocket.

"Howdyado?" Ivy asked.

He gave a small shrug.

She reached out, took the card from his pocket, and flipped it over to the comment section, where he

always excelled. *I adore Ray. Such a kind and trusting boy. He always tries his hardest. What a pleasure to have him in class. I will miss him!!!*

"Three exclamation points," Ivy said. "Three!" Then

she flipped it back to the other side and observed, "Your columns are *loaded* with check-pluses." She registered a small, residual twinge.

"Yeah," he said, as if it were nothing. Neither of them mentioned his grades. "How about you?"

"Original," she told him. "A force. I'm going to make my mark on the world." She handed Ray's card back to him. "We did *good*," she concluded, and she and Ray nodded at each other, satisfied. "Between the two of us," Ivy pointed out, "we got *everything* right!"

They took off then toward the row of doors at the end of the hallway and burst outside into sunshine and fresh air. There was Veddy, waiting, in full uniform, standing at attention next to the limo, which took up nearly three parking spots. He opened the back door for them, and Ray and Ivy shot in across the expanse of leather cushions. They were leaving school behind them with every second that passed, every move they made.

"Your demeanor suggests that against all odds you both achieved promotion," Veddy said as he settled himself into the driver's seat and located them in the rearview mirror.

"Sure we passed!" Ray said, a trifle indignant. "We're not *that* bad!"

Veddy never fooled Ivy anymore. She knew he was teasing.

"Then I believe some culinary satisfaction is called for," he announced, maneuvering the long car out of the school driveway. He took them directly for ice cream sundaes.

Desirable Destinations

Dan Fitts had called the family meeting for 8 p.m. sharp.

"That's at *night*," Ivy reminded Ray, just to show that she knew about p.m.

But Ray didn't have to be told, because they always met on Ray and Ivy's first night of freedom from school; it was a Fitts family tradition.

Shortly before the meeting was to start, Ray and Ivy were upstairs in the bathroom that connected their two bedrooms. They had spent the afternoon constructing and running an obstacle course around the estate, and now they were washing the bottoms of their feet, which were green and brown from mown grass and dirt. All they could talk about was vacation.

Ivy reiterated her position that they needed to go someplace fun. Someplace *not boring*. Ivy thought Carol and Dan had gone downhill as far as having fun was concerned. At Christmastime Carol had decided that colored lights weren't a class act and allowed only white lights on the tree. A few weeks ago Ivy had come home from school to discover that Carol had straightened her hair! All her beautiful curls, gone! As for Dan—ever since his release from prison, all he wanted to do was hole up in the library and research their stupid family history. That was bad enough, but worse was how mad it made Carol. "Him and his family tree," Carol said. "Obviously a *nut* tree!" Ivy didn't know about nuts, but she did worry that poring over dusty old books and birth certificates and death certificates was cramping Dan's style. She thought there were much better ways to have fun. Take a trip, for instance—hit the road. It was Dan himself who had taught her that.

"Chicago," Ivy said, scrubbing a particularly green spot on the bottom of her foot. She liked the idea of a big lake.

"Disneyland," Ray said.

"Been there," Ivy answered. They never went to the same place twice.

"Las Vegas," he tried, but they had been there, too.

"Bora Bora," Ivy said. Her finger had never actually landed there on the globe, but she had seen it go by, and even just saying it—*Bora Bora*—she knew it had to be a good place.

"Hawaii," Ray said, and Ivy agreed that Hawaii would be OK. She did a little hula dance, waving her hands in one direction and then the other.

"Or Alaska," she added. Hawaii and Alaska went together in her mind.

Wherever they went, there were bound to be motels with swimming pools: a top priority for them. Basically, Ivy felt they couldn't lose, whatever place they picked. "C'mon," she said, tossing Ray the towel so he could dry his feet. "It's time."

They were due to meet in the library, the room Dan used as his office. The door was open wide, inviting them in. Dan had straightened up his piles of papers and charts and books and arranged four chairs in a circle. He had, of course, lit candles. Fitts family meetings were always held by candlelight. Ray, Ivy, Carol, and Dan each took a seat—wide leather chairs with gold-headed tacks along the arms, and seats so deep that Ray's legs stuck straight out and Ivy's dangled high above the floor. Carol was wearing her sundress that tied at the back of her neck, and Ivy was pleased to see that her hair was at least trying to be wavy. The candles cast beautiful, promising shadows around the book-lined room. Ivy had a good feeling.

The first thing they did was sing "Mele Kaliki-maka" (... *is the way to say Merry Christmas on a bright Hawaiian day* ...), which was how, for the past few years,

they had kicked things off. As they sang, Ivy had more good thoughts about maybe going to Hawaii.

She assumed the first order of business would be the announcement of their destination, but when the singing was done, Dan started in about his research. His research! "I've unearthed some interesting finds," he told them.

"Un*earthed*?" Ray repeated, hopeful. He was interested in mummies.

"Did you unearth a good *destination*?" Ivy asked. The last thing she wanted to hear about was boring family history.

Carol wasn't saying a word. She had her arms folded and was just watching Dan, waiting.

Suddenly he reached into his pocket and pulled out a large red jewel and held it up to the candlelight. "Look what I found," he said.

All three of them—Ivy, Ray, and Carol—leaned forward in their seats. Carol's hands instantly unfolded, and she fanned her fingers as if a giant ring had just appeared on each of them. As for Ivy, every desirable destination she'd been thinking about flew right out of her head. The stone had her complete and undivided attention. She loved things that sparkled, loved how they caught the light. (Ivy had heard Dan tell the story, more than once, about the first time she had climbed out of her crib all by herself, in quest of a prism on the windowsill that was shooting off rainbow bits of light all over her walls and ceiling. Dan always told the story proudly, as proof that Ivy had an eye worth cultivating.)

"Where'd you *get* it?" Ray asked.

"Found it," Dan answered.

"You *found* it?" Ivy said.

"I did," he told her.

Why hadn't *she*, Ivy wondered, found it? *She* kept her eyes open. *She* snooped. "Where?" she asked, a little indignantly.

Dan's smile broadened. "Right under our noses," he said. "Where most good things are to be found. Family research led me straight to it." He walked over to the wall of books behind him and ran his finger along a row of leather-bound volumes. Midway he stopped and pulled out a book. Even from where she sat, Ivy could read its gold-stamped title: *THE LAST LAUGH*.

Dan brought the book back to their circle, and Ivy reached out for it. She took the volume in her hand, intent on finding any secret it might hold. She examined the fancy gold tooling on the front and back, admired the shine of its gilded pages. She studied the gold stamping between the raised bands on the spine. The title came first, then "Blackstone Mouton," and down at the bottom, "Vol. II." She lifted the book to her face and smelled it, breathed in its leathery aroma. When she opened it, though, she discovered that *The Last Laugh* wasn't a book at all! Its pages were glued together in a solid block, and a hole had been cut into the center. Within that sunken square sat a little velvet bag with a tasseled silk cord.

Ivy drew in her breath. She loved the containers jewels came in almost as much as she loved the jewels—those little velvet bags, in shades of midnight blue or crimson, cinched with twisted cords; boxes that snapped shut on themselves, with clever padded slits for holding rings.

"And *that's* where I found this little, ah, artifact." Dan was once again holding up the jewel. "Which just shows to go ya," he added, "you really *can't* judge a book by its cover."

Ivy didn't know which she liked better—the jewel or the box-in-a-book. She coveted both.

"Let *me* hold it," Ray said to Ivy, but she didn't.

"So what do you suppose it's worth?" Dan asked.

The jewel was pinched between his fingers. Dan had on his poker face, the one that betrayed nothing—no sense of how valuable it might be, this object that caught the light and shone. It reminded Ivy of the big diamond ring Dan had given Carol one Christmas. This was no diamond, though. This jewel was red—a ruby. Ivy checked to see her mother's expression this time around. She was leaning in toward the ruby as if it were a magnet, but looking at Dan with narrow eyes. Ivy knew she was thinking, *What are you up to?*

"A million dollars," Ray called out.

"What about you?" Dan said to Ivy. She stretched her body closer. Dan was testing her, and she didn't want to get it wrong. She *wanted* the ruby to be worth a million, but she didn't want to be gullible. Ray was the gullible one in the family.

Maybe the jewel Dan was holding up to them was

a fake! People fell for fakes all the time. Her father had taught her that there's a sucker born every minute. But she wasn't one of them; she *prided* herself on not being one of them. She wished she had one of those things jewelers put in their eyes to study stones with. Something that would show whether they were real or not, whether they were worth a million bucks or nothing at all.

"Ivy?" Dan prodded her. "What say you?"

"Can I bite it?" she asked. She had seen people do that. Where? In movies, maybe, and she didn't know why people did, exactly. Did real things *taste* different from fakes? And if they did, how would she know which was which?

Dan shook his head. He was waiting for her answer.

"It's a fake," she said—a wild guess.

"Aha!" Dan cried out, and in a flash the jewel he was holding was gone. Poof!

As many times as Ivy had witnessed her father's way of making whatever he happened to be holding in his hand suddenly vanish, it still took Ivy's breath away. She patted the velvet bag inside the box-within-the-book, just in case the ruby had magically reappeared there. She *knew* it hadn't, but she couldn't help checking. And just as she'd suspected, the bag was empty. She closed the cover and pushed the book under her leg, so that it, too, wouldn't disappear. Now that the ruby was gone, Ivy felt sure it *was* worth a million. Why was that? Why did things seem more valuable as soon as they went missing?

Suddenly Dan shook out his hands—a little fireworks of fingers—and then settled back in his seat. He flashed a beautiful smile, bright even in the candlelight. "It remains to be seen what that gem is worth," he said. "But enough of that," he continued. "Let's talk about what else my meticulous research has unearthed, and how we might spend our summer vacation. How's a little road trip sound?"

Ah, *road trip*: the words were music to Ivy's ears. Names and places came flowing back to her. What would it be? Chattanooga? Walla Walla? Constantinople? The Garden of Eden?

"I'm thinking it's high time we met our one remaining distant relative," Dan said. "Have ourselves a family reunion."

What? Ivy's mouth opened, but nothing came out for a second. "Family?" she finally croaked. "*What family?" The only family she counted was the one sitting right there in the circle: Dan and Carol and Ray and her. There was Grampa Blackie—who had pulled off the biggest bank robbery in the history of California!—but he was dead. And their great-grandfather Blackstone Mouton, who'd given them the inheritance but whom they'd never known. He was dead, too. Oh, and Marietta and Lionel. Ivy always tried to forget they were related. Marietta was the one who had sent Dan and Carol to prison last time and who had tried to swindle her and Ray out of their inheritance.

"So glad you asked," Dan said, rising from his chair and stepping behind the desk. From high up on the wall he pulled down two screens. On the top one he had sketched out a big, black family tree. Names and dates and connecting lines hung off the branches like ugly ornaments.

Ivy's heart sank.

"Family," Dan said solemnly. "The tie that binds. What it all comes down to in the end. Not to mention a treasure trove of stories."

Ivy considered herself something of an expert when it came to good stories, and none of her favorites were about family history.

"And it turns out we've got more of a family than we

thought," Dan continued. "I've discovered a long-lost cousin—Gladys—currently residing in Florida."

"Florida!" Ray shouted. It was one of the places he and Ivy had put on their list.

Ivy pictured, in her mind's eye, the squiggly little leg it extended off the bottom of the United States—but she was still wary. "Cousin?" she said. She'd never heard anything about a cousin before.

"Twice removed," Dan qualified.

Ivy couldn't remember if that meant sent to jail two times or sent to two different jails. And she didn't want to ask in case it seemed like she didn't know.

"Our age?" she asked. She wasn't about to fritter away their vacation stuck with a *baby*.

"Actually she's elderly," Dan continued. "Which is all the more reason to meet her now. While she's still around."

"Why?" Ray asked. "Where's she going?"

Ivy's first thought was that she might be going back to prison. But that would make her thrice removed. "She's going to die," Ivy answered. "Right?" she asked Dan, just to check.

"Afraid so," Dan said, who didn't sound a bit afraid. "We shouldn't dawdle if we're going to meet her and present her with the Mouton family heirloom."

Carol's fingers recoiled as if they'd been burned. "The *relative* gets the ruby?" she said. She choked a bit and then started to cough.

Ray patted her on the back.

"A token of our affection," Dan explained. "A peace offering to end old family feuds. Research reveals that she and Blackstone parted on bad terms ... and she hasn't been heard from since."

Carol leaned forward. "I say let sleeping dogs lie."

Dan shook his head. "She's part of our family, our history. Plus she must be a gold mine of information," he said. His eyes glistened.

Why give a gold mine a ruby, Ivy wondered.

"I move that we go to Florida," Dan continued. "Anyone want to second a road trip to find Gladys and present her with the Mouton family heirloom?"

Ray's and Ivy's hands shot up. Ivy had her doubts about extended family, but she and Ray *always* seconded Dan's moves.

"Where will we stay?" Ray asked happily, clearly on board.

"Another fine question," Dan responded, and pulled on the family tree so that it rolled up on itself, revealing a map underneath. Pinheads of different colors made an S-shaped path along the eastern coast. "I figure we can meander south, visit some friends, see some sights, eventually end up with old Gladys in the Everglades, and then make a beeline back home." He drew an imaginary road straight up the pinhead path. "And seeing as how she's family and all," Dan said, "only seems right we should stay with her."

"*With* her!" Disappointment saturated Ivy. What good

was a road trip without motels—without swimming pools and ice machines down the hall? She wanted little bars of soap wrapped in paper. The good feeling she'd had at the start of the meeting was slipping away. Who wanted more family members anyway? Marietta and Lionel hadn't been such great additions. Would some distant relative twice removed be any better? The odds were against it, Ivy thought. Dan had taught her to calculate the odds.

Ivy turned to Ray and then to Carol to see how they were taking the news. Maybe they could put it to a vote, or at least, as a united front, have some sway about accommodations. But Carol had gone back to studying her hands, her long, painted nails, as if they were the only things that existed in the world. And Ray was grinning like mad. Didn't anyone but Ivy care that the plan for their summer vacation was questionable?

But then Ivy saw *why* Ray was grinning, and had to forgive him: Dan was getting out the squirt guns. He had them filled in advance. He handed Ray an orange one; Ivy's was blue. Then he lifted the two tallest candles in their holders and moved them to the threshold of the library door. "Who fires first?"

Ivy and Ray did a quick rock-paper-scissors, and Ray won—scissors cut paper.

He centered himself in his seat and took careful aim.
His first squirt shot close to the top of the flame and
made it waver. His second was off by a mile. His third
hit its mark, but not with enough water to douse it.

Then it was Ivy's turn. She loved it when it was. She
extended her right arm and with her left hand gripped
her wrist and steadied the hand that held the squirt
gun. She closed one eye (something she had always
been proud of being able to do) and sighted the flame
and took careful aim. She pulled back the trigger hard
and fast, and her squirt of water went flying toward its
mark. She fired again as soon as she could. Plenty of

water was the secret to success. Her third squirt did the trick: the candle went out.

Ray jumped up from his chair and cheered, as pleased as if he'd done it himself. Ivy loved that about Ray. She saw her father give his quick nod of approval.

"I win," she said. Winning softened the disappointment she had felt just a minute before. Everything seemed a little better, a little easier to accept, with a victory in her pocket. "So you're sure about this family reunion plan ... ?" she asked, inviting reassurance.

"Sure as shootin'," Dan told her. He leaned down to face her, eye to eye. "Trust me," he said. Then he went behind the desk and pressed the buzzer that was hidden beneath the carpet. A minute later Marietta entered, toting a tray loaded with mugs of hot chocolate and a large angel food cake. They had angel food cake at the end of every family meeting. It was a Fitts family favorite.

THE PLOT SICKENS

Late that night, Ray and Ivy held their own after-meeting meeting, in the big claw-foot bathtub in the bathroom that connected their bedrooms. They shut both doors to ensure privacy, and then Ray took his place at the end with

the faucets and Ivy leaned against the sloped back. The family meeting had ended on a good note, and now she had a surprise of her own to spring on Ray: she had smuggled *The Last Laugh* out of the library after they finished their cake. It seemed only fair to her that she and Ray should have it, seeing as how Dan had the ruby. She opened it once again to reveal the carved-out hole, the lovely, empty velvet bag and tassel.

"*Now* can I see it?" Ray asked.

Reluctantly she handed the book over. He might have praised her accomplished smuggling a bit more, she thought. But as Ray examined the prize, Ivy settled into bigger thoughts. "So what do *you* think it is?" she finally asked.

Ray's eyes got rounder. "What *what* is?" he said.

"The *plan*," Ivy answered. "Obviously Dan has a plan," she told her younger brother.

Ray shrugged. "Family reunion," he said.

"Oh, Ray, this isn't about a family reunion," Ivy said assuredly. "It's about the ruby."

Ray didn't respond right away. Then he said, "We get to go to Florida! Florida's good."

"What's Florida got to do with anything?" Ivy said.

Ray shrugged. "It was on our list," he tried.

"Ray," Ivy said, "I'm not talking about *where*. I'm talking about *what*—what's up. The real story."

"He *said* it's a family reunion." Sometimes Ray persisted.

But that explanation was way too simple. Ivy preferred more complicated, more exciting reasons for why things were the way they were. "No, something's *up*," she repeated. "And it could be dangerous," she threw in. She reached down and took the leather volume back from him.

"You jump to conclusions," Ray said. He had learned that expression in school, and he applied it to Ivy on a regular basis. He started fitting his fingers between his toes.

"I do not!" Ivy said, sitting up in the tub. She didn't

44

like it when Ray—or anyone—said things about her that weren't great.

"You do too." Ray stuck to his guns. His narrow shoulders rose and fell in a quick shrug. "You jump to conclusions."

"Well, *you're* gullible," she countered. Gullible was something Ivy never wanted to be.

He didn't respond for a second. Then he said, "Maybe Gladys will have a pool." He always returned to simple pleasures. "Or maybe we can go fishing."

It was true that Dan often called their trips "fishing expeditions." But Ivy didn't think Dan was really interested in fish. "We have to be on the lookout," she announced. "For danger signs!" Oooh, she liked the sound of those words: *danger signs*. "We need to start a list," she declared. Ivy and Ray often drew up lists during their meetings.

"I'll get the notebook." Ray hopped out of the tub and went burrowing in the cabinet where the extra toilet paper and folded towels were stacked—behind which they kept their own supplies: the notebook, pencils, a flashlight, graham crackers.

Ray delivered the spiral-bound pad to Ivy, and she placed it on top of *The Last Laugh*, against her drawn-up

45

knees. She opened it to their most recent list—Desirable Destinations. The one before that was Prose and Cons—they had spent a rainy-day meeting evaluating Carol after she had insisted on white-only Christmas lights.

Ivy threw back those pages and smoothed a fresh, blank sheet of paper beneath her hand. She licked the tip of her pencil, the way secretaries did in the old movies she watched with Dan, and then, at the top, she wrote *DANGER SINS*.

#1. mor family.

#2. ruby—real or fake?

#3. Carol mad

"She *is*?" Ray said. He sat up straight, at attention. "What's she mad about?"

Ivy wasn't sure. Sometimes it was hard to tell with Carol. A lot of things made her mad. She clearly wasn't pleased that Gladys was getting the ruby. And she wasn't crazy about all that family history and research Dan was doing. "Stuff," Ivy answered, hoping Ray would let it slide.

Ray slumped down a little in the tub. Ivy continued

to think of danger signs. After a minute Ray asked, his head tilting to the side as he read, "What's *V-O-L-I-I*?"

"What?"

He tapped the spine of *The Last Laugh*, where the gold letters were stamped.

"Volume Two," Ivy answered, glad to have learned about Roman numerals before he did.

"Oh," Ray said.

"Volume *Two*!" Ivy suddenly repeated, and now *she* sat straight up in the tub. "Which means ... there's a Volume *One*!"

"So?" Ray said.

"So we should get it," Ivy announced.

"Why?"

"Because!" she answered as she climbed out of the tub. "Look what Dan found in Volume Two! Volume One could be a gold mine!" Her mind raced with possibilities, all manner of hidden treasure. "Let's sneak down and get it."

The mention of sneaking always brought Ray around one hundred percent. He flung his leg over the side of the tub.

"I'll get the flashlight," Ivy said. She burrowed through layers of terry cloth in the cabinet.

Ray disappeared into his room to get his sneaking socks. He had taken to wearing a particular pair of socks when he and Ivy snuck up on people or investigated places. He thought they absorbed the creaks in stairs and muffled the sound of footsteps.

Ivy found Ray's theory preposterous. She was a firm believer in bare feet. But she never teased him about the socks because he was so convinced. "You have the courage of your convictions," she told him once, after she had learned that expression in school.

He and Ivy met in the hallway and descended the back staircase into the kitchen. The dishwasher was on, clicking and gushing. What remained of the angel food cake sat on a flowered dish beneath a tin cover. They took a quick detour over to the counter, lifted the cover, and pinched off pieces before they tiptoed on to the library. Dan and Carol had gone to bed, and the downstairs was dark and closed up. They could have turned on a lamp or two but preferred to follow the narrow beam their flashlight provided.

In no time at all they were standing where they had been only a while earlier, but now, because it was dark and late, the library seemed an entirely different place—almost ghostly, Ivy thought. The chairs were still gathered in a circle, but no one was in them. Book-lined shelves, silent and mysterious, surrounded her and Ray. Ivy studied them with new appreciation now that she had seen for herself the hidden treasure a book could contain.

"Where was it?" Ray whispered.

Ivy made a beeline to the exact place Dan had plucked it from. She found Vol. I almost immediately, jimmied her fingers around its spine, and pulled it off the shelf. The leather felt smooth and rich; the gold lettering on the spine glittered even in the weak light. She wanted to fling back the cover then and there but made herself wait, to draw out the thrill.

"C'mon," she said. "Back to the tub." She handed the flashlight to Ray. "You point it." She wanted to walk very straight and tall, to carry the book like a precious tablet.

Ray took the light and waved it wildly around the room. "Let's get more cake," he said.

Was food all Ray thought about? Ivy wondered. Even when they might be hot on the trail of a price-less jewel? Still, she followed the path he shone straight back to the angel food cake and helped Ray finish off every last crumb. Then she resumed her regal posture and they tiptoed up the stairs. Moments later they had reconvened in the bathtub.

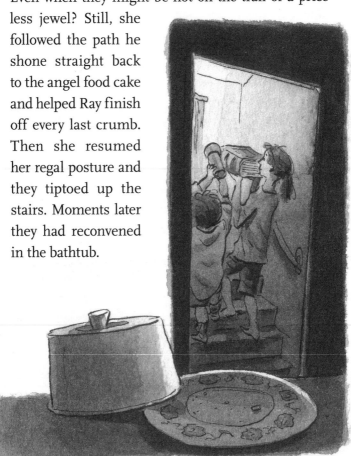

Ivy cradled the book in her hands. She pinched the cover between her fingers. What would she discover? A diamond? A sapphire? A bag of gold coins? Very slowly she opened it.

And there she found—all she found—was a book: an actual, regular, real book. Large black type on the first page proclaimed THE LAST LAUGH, and beneath that, in letters almost as large, *Blackstone Mouton II*.

"Where's the treasure?" Ray asked.

Ivy quickly turned the first page, only to reveal another, and then another, and then another. She flipped through all the pages, back to front. They shuffled beneath her thumb without a hitch, each one separate and free, nothing glued to anything else. She lifted up the back cover in the hope of finding a hidden compart-  ment there, but that revealed only the same marbled endpapers as in the front. She clapped the book shut and held it at arm's length. "It's all words," she said, disgusted.

Once again she opened it, as if giving it a second chance to be something other than what it was, something better. And once again it was only a book, front, back, and in between, and she shut it with an angry snap.

They were silent for a moment. Then Ray said, "Maybe it's written in code."

Ray and his ideas! Just the same, she opened it and glanced at a page. It was filled with boring, everyday, real words.

No, they had to face it: Vol. I was a book and nothing but a book. A disappointment, to be sure, but Ivy was not about to declare their sneaking and smuggling mission a failure. "At least we have a ..." She searched for the best word she could think of. "Story," she said.

Ray looked unimpressed.

"We can read it," she said. "And find out things."

"*Read* it?" he repeated, weakly.

Ray wasn't so big on reading, and Ivy knew it. "Maybe he tells where to find more jewels," she offered. "Or secrets. Books aren't *all* bad." She herself had learned a thing or two from them. "Let's adjourn the meeting and I'll read to you in bed."

Ray liked that idea.

"One last thing, though," Ivy said before officially

declaring their meeting over, and she added #4 to her list of Danger Sins: "a real book."

A few minutes later, they were changed into their pj's and propped up by pillows in Ray's bed. Ivy held *The Last Laugh*, Vol. I, in her lap. She told herself it would still be just a book when she opened it, but once again she hoped. Lifting the cover and seeing only pages, Ivy consoled herself with announcing, "I knew it." Then she began to read.

"*The Last Laugh*, by Blackstone Mouton ..."—she started to say "Eye Eye" but remembered about Roman numerals and caught herself. "Two," she said, and then "The Second." She and Ray examined the oval portrait of Blackstone Mouton II on the facing page. It brought to mind George Washington—turned to the side, looking stern and important in the picture of him in her history book. Next came the table of contents, and finally, after that, the beginning: "*It is my great good fortune, indeed, to descend from so illustrious and accomplished a line of ancestors, many of whom have altered the very face of history. I have endeavored, in my own humble way, to follow in their footsteps ...*"

Ivy was bored before she even got to the end of the

paragraph. It was worse than the stuff they got handed in school. "How can Dan *read* this?" she said.

Ray was already half-asleep. She flipped back to the table of contents, to see if any of the chapter titles looked more promising. Chapter 5, she saw, was called "Rubies, the Stepping Stones to My Fortune." She turned to page 102, cleared her throat, and tried again: *"Gems were the stepping stones to my great fortune, and in my youth I played an important role—if I do say so myself—in elevating the availability of rubies through careful selection, distribution, and presentation ..."* Ivy read on, quickly. A little farther down, buried in the next paragraph, was the one line that actually interested her: *"My one and only regret regarding this time in my life concerns the unfortunate association with my business partner—and distant relative—Gladys Mouton. Never do business with a relative!"* Ivy gave Ray's ribs a swift jab with her elbow.

"What?" he said, shooting up off the pillow.

"Listen to *this*," she said, and read on: *"I exposed Gladys to a wide range of creative business opportunities and ventures. And how was I rewarded for my generosity? I am grieved to say that she absconded with the centerpiece of my fortune!"*

"She absconded!" Ivy repeated, not entirely sure of its meaning but convinced of its dramatic content. "With the centerpiece!" Ivy said. "Of his *fortune*!"

Ray snuggled back down under the covers.

"So *that's* it," Ivy declared.

"That's what?" Ray said. He was struggling to stay awake.

"What this trip is really about—Blackstone's fortune that Gladys absconded!" A satisfied moment later, she declared, "The plot sickens," just the way Dan often did when he came upon interesting information. She felt a pang then for having doubted Dan. She should have known he would never subject them to a boring family vacation.

Off Like a Herd of Turtles

Only minutes later, it seemed, Dan was leaning over Ray and Ivy, shaking them awake. The sun hadn't even come up yet. It was hard for Ivy to leave the dream that was unfolding beneath her eyelids, in which she played a starring role. Archibald Ames couldn't spell for beans, but Ivy could; she could spell perfectly.

"Time to go," Dan crooned. He gave her shoulder a gentle shake. "Let's saddle up." Finally his words broke through the championship spelling bee Ivy was winning. "Hit the road," she heard Dan say, and she awoke. She stumbled out of bed. Ray was already standing, rubbing his eyes, his hair all poking up.

Being up before dawn in the cool, dim limbo between night and day felt wonderfully unfamiliar, planets away from a regular school day. Plus things from the evening before were beginning to resurface: *the ruby, the secret volume, summer vacation.* Ivy hurried to her room to dress. *Absconded.* She fetched her suitcases and began packing. Dan had taught them all how to travel light and fast. Ivy knew he would have the car waiting, and they would make a smooth getaway.

She crumpled up her pajamas, tossed them into her suitcase, and snapped it shut. She called out to Ray not to forget his pillow. Suddenly *The Last Laugh*—both volumes—appeared in her mind like images in a dream. She had shoved them under Ray's bed before falling asleep, and now she hotfooted it back to his room and fished them out, along with their spiral-bound notebook of lists. She tossed the notebook to Ray and told him to bring it along for their meetings on the road. After allowing herself one last peek at the delicious hidden compartment inside Vol. II, she declared—as much to herself as to Ray—"We have to put these back." She was wide awake now, and aware of the need to cover their tracks. Dan had taught her that. She had also learned the hard way, having been caught a few times holding things that weren't hers.

Toting their suitcases, pillows, and one volume

each, Ivy and Ray made their way down the back stairs, retracing their steps from the night before but omitting the detour to the cake, since they had already eaten it all. Ivy quickly reshelved the books in the library, and they slipped into the grand entry hall and from there out to the porch.

Veddy had driven the limo around to the front of the house and was standing beside it—as if, Ivy thought, he had been standing there all night, just waiting for them.

Dan was loading his duffle bag into the trunk. This would be, Ivy realized, their first road trip ever without Dan behind

the wheel. Over the years, Ivy had seen him drive all kinds of vehicles—one year they took their road trip in a double-decker bus, once it was a Cadillac with big fins, and they made their drive to Reno, Nevada, in a hearse. But now that they had Veddy and the limo, why would they travel any other way? You couldn't do much better than a limo stocked with soda and candy and a driver who wore a uniform.

Dan bounded up the steps and relieved them of their suitcases. "Allow me," he said. If not being the driver bothered him, it sure didn't show. He was flashing his million-dollar smile. "Ready?" he asked them.

"Ready," Ivy and Ray answered in unison, and leading with their pillows they climbed into the limo.

Where was Carol? Ivy had a sudden flash of Carol's straightened hair, remembered her shudder when Dan said the ruby was going to Gladys. She hoped Carol wouldn't put the kibosh on their adventure before it even began.

But then, suddenly, there she was, sweeping in behind them, climbing into the limo, dressed in a wide, full skirt and high-heeled sandals, wearing perfume, making what she would have called "a perfect entrance." Ivy watched Carol settle herself in the seat directly behind the glass partition, lower the sun visor, and check her face in the little mirror that was attached. And even though she knew she was looking at her mother, Ivy imagined that she was watching a movie: a movie about a movie star—a beautiful, rich woman sitting in a limousine, pursing her lips and turning her face to a certain angle, preparing herself for the best the world had to offer.

Having Carol arrive so fully, in such a glamorous way, gave their trip a rosy beginning. Ivy looked out the window and saw the sky turning a glorious spreading pink. Her elbow rose automatically and she poked it into Ray's ribs. "Look," she told him, jutting her chin outward. "We beat the sun." She scrunched her pillow behind her head and leaned back, satisfied that they were off to a good start and sure that whatever was up would at least not be boring.

Moments after they cleared the winding driveway, Ivy asked, "So what's our first stop?" It was understood that she was asking about the first stop *after breakfast*, because they always stopped for breakfast at the first place they could all agree on.

"First stop," Dan said, stretching out his long legs, "will be Wolfgang's."

"What?" Carol yelped, just as Ray and Ivy repeated the name in chorus: "Wolfgang?" Then, in honor of the name, they clenched their teeth and growled at each other.

"Wolfgang? Is that someone's real name?" Ivy asked.

"Yep. Wolfgang Mann." He pronounced *Mann* as if it rhymed with *con*. "I got to know Wolfie when I was away," Dan explained.

When Dan said he was away, he meant when he was in prison, and hearing that word—*away*—always gave Ivy a funny feeling, like going down fast in an elevator.

"We were thick as thieves," Dan continued, "before we both went straight."

Carol let out a dry little laugh that didn't sound happy. Her hair was hanging like a curtain, Ivy thought, on either side of her face.

Dan changed the subject. "How about we eat at the Country Kitchen?"

When it came to restaurants, they all had their own preferences. Ray opted for places likely to serve chocolate-chip pancakes. Ivy always hoped for jukeboxes—preferably one at every table. Carol just wanted a place with "a little class."

The Country Kitchen sounded to Ivy like the kind of place that would serve oatmeal. "Boring," she said, and so they drove on past. Around the next bend, though, they came upon the Close-to-Home Restaurant, which no one vetoed. Veddy maneuvered the limo into the parking lot and dropped everyone off.

"A captain stays with his ship," Dan explained to Ivy and Ray, as he did whenever they begged Veddy, just for once, to join them.

On the steps up to the restaurant Ivy found a long black feather with rows of white spots. Once they had snagged the corner booth—the best seats in the house,

Dan said—Ivy made Ray guess how many white dots there were. She was still counting them when the waitress came to take their orders. Her hair made Ivy think of wet black ink.

In no time at all she was bringing them everything they wanted. Ivy admired how she could carry plates balanced all the way up her arm. When she served Ray his pancakes she said, "Here you go, doll," and after that Ivy called Ray "doll," too, until he told her to "quit it, poison Ivy."

Ray and Ivy ate fast and finished first and were ready to buy some Life Savers at the counter and hit the road again. But Carol and Dan ordered another

cup of coffee. Ray and Ivy looked at each other and sighed, then decided to go to the bathroom to kill time. They followed the painted wooden hands with a pointing finger that said *Restrooms* into a darker, narrow corridor, to two separate doors—one with a chicken on it, the other with a rooster. The rooster door also had a sign that said *Gents*, so Ivy was able to announce, with complete authority, "That's yours."

They leaned back against their respective doors but didn't go in—just stood, facing each other. Ivy plucked the feather from her belt loop and brushed it smooth against her leg. She held it up to Ray. "What do you think *it's* worth?" They had already determined that it had sixty-seven spots.

"Are feathers worth *any*thing?" he asked.

"They must be," she said. "They're beautiful." She held the feather at its tip and twirled it back and forth. "Beauty counts," she ruled.

"At least to birds," Ray said. "But they don't have money."

"Money's not everything," Ivy said—she had heard that somewhere—but a moment later she asked, "If the ruby *was* worth a million dollars, what would you do with it?"

"The ruby?"

"No, the money! What would you do with the million bucks?"

Ray shrugged before he answered. "Another vacation?" he said.

"We could take as many as we wanted," Ivy pointed

out. "To *anywhere.*" She was picturing aqua blue water and little huts with thatched roofs.

Ray's voice intruded. "School, though," he said.

Ivy registered a thud. The Student-of-the-Year disappointment still rankled a bit. She wondered—could you *buy* your way out of going to school?

"Besides," Ray continued, "I thought we were giving it to Gladys for a present."

"Oh, Ray," Ivy said. "Didn't you listen to what I read last night? Gladys absconded!" How sweet it still sounded to her. "This trip's not about one little ruby. We're after the centerpiece ... of a fortune!"

"Dan *said*—" Ray started, but Ivy cut him off.

"It's not what people say that matters," she told him. "It's what they do." Teachers—more than one—had told her that at school.

They were both quiet then. Ivy went back to twirling the feather, trying to hypnotize herself with it.

"Why's he called Wolf?" Ray said. "Gang."

"No accounting for taste," Ivy answered him—that was something Carol often said. "Maybe his parents liked the name."

"Do you think he could be?" Ray asked.

"Be what?"

"A werewolf?" Ray said.

"A werewolf!" Ivy repeated, twice as loud. She stilled the feather. "Is *that* what you think? That we're on our way to a werewolf's?"

"No," Ray answered quickly, quietly. Ivy saw a blush creeping up his neck, into his ears.

"Just because someone's name is Wolfgang doesn't mean he's a werewolf." She spoke, as always, with complete authority.

"I *know*," Ray said again. "I was just kidding."

"Right," Ivy started, and then stopped. Sometimes Ray had bogus ideas, but embarrassing him about them didn't appeal to Ivy. Once—or twice—she'd had a mistaken idea herself, when she was little. She tucked the feather back in her belt loop. "Carol thinks Wolfgang's a bad influence," she told Ray, "but not because he's a werewolf."

They were quiet for a second more—a silence into which Ray's question of werewolves could simply dissolve—and then Ivy leaned harder against her bathroom door. "See ya later, Wolfie," she said.

"Sayonara, Wolfgang," he answered, cracking open his rooster door.

One step into the chicken restroom and everything smelled like cherry syrup. Ivy loved that smell. Plus there were the good hand dryers that blew hot air. She pressed the silver button repeatedly and warmed various parts of her body in the tunnel of wind. She thought some more about Ray's funny idea that Wolfgang could be a werewolf. She knew he wasn't a werewolf. No way.

She didn't even believe in were-wolves, for the most part, and never during the day. But now that she thought about it, who *was* Wolfie, anyway? And what kind of name was that—Wolf-gang? And why had Carol sat up so straight at the mention of his name? The hot air shut off and the bathroom got quiet and Ivy stayed for a moment longer, pondering.

By the time she and Ray had slid back into their places in the booth, Dan and Carol had already signaled the waitress that they were finally done. Then Carol said it was her turn to use the ladies' room, and Ivy stuck her hands into her armpits, flapped her arms, and started clucking. Carol didn't ask why; Ivy and Ray slid low on the seats of the booth, laughing.

Sunlight glinted through the windows and made diamonds on the Formica tabletop. Now that they had Dan all to themselves, Ivy couldn't resist asking about the jewel. "What *is* it worth?" Ivy said. "The ruby."

Dan's eyebrows lifted. Interest raised the corners of his mouth. He was clearly pleased that Ivy had brought it up. "Are you referring to the Mouton family heirloom?" he said. He scratched behind his ear, and the next thing Ivy knew, she was looking at it: pinched between his fingers, in front of her face. Out of nowhere.

It was a beauty. Up close, in the daylight, Ivy could see that. And big. Instinctively she put out her hand to take it, but Dan didn't let go. "What *is* it worth?" she asked again.

"Worth?" Dan repeated, as if its value had never crossed his mind. "Well," he said, "they say beauty is in the eye of the beholder. They say a bird in the hand is worth two in the bush. They say there's no such thing as a free lunch."

"We just had *breakfast*," Ray pointed out.

"What do *you* say?" Ivy pleaded. She really cared only about that.

"I say its worth remains to be seen," Dan said. "I say we're on our way to find out. But, you know, you can't put a price tag on some things—like a family heirloom."

"Or a feather!" Ivy said, and held up her spotted treasure.

POISON

Back in the parking lot, Ivy showed her found feather to Veddy and thrilled to his suggestion that they place it at the front tip of the limo, wedged beside the silver hoodie. Ivy felt that it gave the limo even greater glory—announced them, somehow, as they wound their way along the country road. Dan had told Veddy to take the scenic route. Back roads offered more possibilities, he said, and you could never have too many of those.

Veddy sailed the limo along as if they owned the road—which, to a certain extent, Ivy felt, they did. They drove for hours and saw a number of things worth noting: a dead possum, an old billboard pockmarked from buckshot, and a huge wooden ice cream cone with colored sprinkles painted on it, nailed to a tree with a big arrow beneath it. It was a rule, on Fitts family road trips, that they could stop for ice cream as many times as anyone wanted to. "Hang a right," Dan called out to Veddy the instant they spotted it, and two minutes later all of them but Carol and Veddy were ordering two-scoop cones with jimmies.

Once they were back on the road, it became clear to Ivy that something wasn't sitting right with Carol. She didn't join in the poker game Dan got going, and after a while she said she wasn't feeling all that well and stretched out on the long leather seat. "It's probably nothing," she said, turning her face away.

After a few rounds of poker, Dan bowed out too, and Ivy and Ray switched to playing Ivy's favorite game: I Doubt It. Ivy shuffled, then made a bridge of the cards and let them cascade down. She loved the waterfall sound they made and how grown-up she felt doing it.

Ray cut the deck and Ivy dealt. She drew up her cards close to her chest, just the way Dan had taught her. She pinched the bottoms of them tightly and spread them into a narrow fan. Ray, across from her, held his cards wide, loose, and low until Dan reminded him not to share his hand with the world.

"Go," Ivy told him.

"One ace," Ray said, choosing a card and placing it face down between them.

"I doubt it," Ivy said—one of her favorite expressions.

He flipped over the card and handed it to her: an ace it was.

"Three twos," Ivy said, and no sooner had she placed down a nine, a seven, and the ace she had just picked up than Carol shot up and cried out, "Stop!" Ivy froze as if she'd been caught in her bluff, but Carol meant the car. Dan leaned forward to tell Veddy, who pulled over to the side. Carol made a mad dash out the door

before Veddy could even get around to open it for her, and went plowing into the bushes along the side of the road. Ray and Ivy watched open-mouthed from the car and listened as their mother threw up.

Ray and Ivy looked at each other. "*Gross,*" they said at the same time.

"She should've had a cone," Ivy added. No one would throw up ice cream, she figured.

When Carol was done and standing up straight, Ivy thought she looked small and even a little fragile, like a china doll, with her wide skirt sticking out straight around her.

Dan was waiting a few feet to the side and took her elbow and helped her back into the limo. This entrance wasn't anything like the one she'd made before dawn. Now she was all white and shaky and her skirt was wrinkled, and when she sat down she didn't do any primping at all. She burped.

Dan got a bottle of water from the little refrigerator in the limo, but she shook her head when he held it out to her.

Ray and Ivy just stared. What was Carol doing, being sick? She never had been before, not that Ivy could remember. Carol was the one who *brought* ginger ale and saltines, not the one who *needed* them. And *no* one got sick on vacation—ever.

"Are you *OK*?" Ray finally said.

Responding to Ray made Carol go all soft. "Oh, baby, don't worry," she said. "My stomach's just a little upset."

"What's it upset about?" he said.

"Probably food poisoning," she answered, her pretty face pale and sweaty.

Poison! The word ricocheted inside Ivy's head. She knew a thing or two about poison. She'd seen some movies; she'd read some books. And simply because her name was Ivy, she'd had to endure endless stupid jokes people made connecting poison ... and, well, Ivy. She'd actually grown a little sensitive on the subject.

"I knew we should have gone to that Country Kitchen place instead," Carol said.

Now Ivy felt doubly panged, for her veto. But how could she have known that Close-to-Home would poison her mother? Ivy conjured up the inky-haired waitress in her mind. The rat, she thought. What had Carol ever done to *her*?

"I'll be better now," Carol said weakly, and stretched out on the leather cushions.

Ivy, Ray, and Dan stared at Carol lying there, her hand against her forehead. After a few minutes, though, when it was clear that there was nothing to be done for her, Ivy and Ray returned, a little sheepishly, to cards.

"Your turn," Ivy prodded Ray. He still had the chance to doubt her, but she knew he wouldn't. He never did.

"One three," he said, pulling out a card from his dwindling hand.

"I doubt it," Ivy said reflexively.

Ray turned over his card—a three—and handed her the pile in the middle.

"It wouldn't kill you to bluff once in a while," she told him.

He shrugged. "You just like to doubt," he said.

"That's the *point*," she said. "Doubt."

"Yeah, but you doubt everything," he said.

"I do not!" Ivy said. How she hated criticism. "*You* exaggerate."

"Stop," Carol cried out, springing up. Once again Ivy thought Carol was admonishing *her*, but Veddy knew better and pulled over immediately. In a flash Carol was out the door and retching in the bushes.

Ray and Ivy laid down their hands.

This time, when Carol came back from her trip to the bushes, she simply curled up on the seat and groaned.

That was when Dan suggested that they find a motel sooner rather than later, so Carol could rest up. And moments after he had floated the idea they saw a sign for the True Vu Motel and Cottages. Barely a mile up the road Ivy spotted the L-shaped motel with the flat roof, and the sprinkling of small, white, slightly leaning cottages over to the side. Carol didn't even raise her head to look—which Ivy considered a stroke of luck, since it wasn't the kind of place Carol would have called classy. Ivy was sorry that Carol was sick, but when they turned into the U-turn drive of the True Vu Motel, the blue water of its swimming pool visible even from the road, Ivy couldn't help it—her heart soared.

Carol stayed resting in the limo and Veddy stood guard while Dan went to register them and Ray and Ivy ran around back to check out the pool. It was perfectly empty of swimmers, perfectly blue. No slide, but a diving board, and lounge chairs and an umbrella over to the side. The black lines at the bottom of the pool looked wavy and undulating, like hula-dancer hands beckoning them in. It was all Ivy could do not to take the plunge then and there, clothes and all. But she restrained herself, and she and Ray tore back to the limo to grab their suitcases out of the trunk.

"There's a pool!" Ray leaned inside the car to tell Carol.

Ivy heard a wan "That's nice" float out from the limo as she opened the door to the office and came up behind Dan.

"Did you get our room?" she asked.

The man behind the desk was round-faced and bald. There was a TV on in the corner and a noisy fan moving back and forth, blowing a hot breeze.

"Kids stay free," he said to Dan. "But it's extra for cots."

Ivy loved cots. "I get one!" she cried.

"Me too," Ray said, right behind her.

Dan was peeling off bills from the folded wad of money he kept in a clip. There was a dusty gumball machine by the door, and Ivy asked Dan for quarters. He fished in his pocket and handed some over.

Ivy got a pinkish red ball; Ray's was blue. "Should we get one for Carol?" he asked.

"Bad idea," Ivy told him. She remembered how she

felt when she got sick to her stomach: she didn't want to even hear food mentioned. "Maybe later," she added, because she thought he was nice to think of it at all.

Their room was #119, around back. Dan handed Ivy the key and let her unlock the door. She was good at unlocking things. The drapes were drawn, so when they first walked in she felt as if she were entering a cave. It had that motel smell she liked so much, the one that went along with vacations and small soaps and bottles of shampoo. Dan said he'd go get Carol and left Ray and Ivy to check out the bed, which they found still had some jump left in it, and the little refrigerator, the television, the glasses with paper caps on them—everything was perfect.

And the pool awaited them. They got out their suits and changed. Ivy was right on the verge of calling out "I win" when Ray opened the bathroom door and stepped out in his trunks. Then, just as they were about to leave, Dan and Carol showed up, and the sight of their poor, sick mother stopped them cold.

They parted and she walked between them and dropped down on the bed. "What a dump," she said, but halfheartedly.

Ivy watched Dan's eyebrows go up and then down as

he let out a thin whistle. He told Ray and Ivy that Veddy could be their lifeguard and motioned for them to go.

Ivy was glad to be released. She didn't like seeing Carol sick, since she didn't know what to do about it and she didn't like not knowing what to do. "C'mon," she told Ray, but she had to kind of pull him away, and then he walked slowly, a step behind her.

"How come Carol had to get poisoned?" he asked. His face was pinched.

Ivy turned around. The sun beat down on them. Weeds were pushing up through the cracks in the sidewalk. Ivy was trying to remember everything in the world she knew about poison. Although she considered herself something of an expert on the subject, there had never been an actual poisoning in their family before (unless you counted the time Dan got stung by a jellyfish when they were swimming in South Carolina, and that really didn't seem the same). Suddenly she got an idea. A big one.

"What?" Ray said.

"Someone's out to *get* us," she said.

"They are?" Ray said, all eyes.

Ivy was picturing the inky-haired waitress. Or maybe it was Wolfie? Ivy remembered how her mother had shot up at the mention of his name. "It's so *obvious*," she said. "People don't just all of a sudden get poisoned. Out of nowhere. On *vacation*. Unless they have something really valuable … like …"

"A ruby!" Ray chimed in.

"Exactly. We're after a fortune and they're after us! It could have been any one of us who got poisoned! Maybe we're next, Ray! You and me!"

Ray was taking in every word Ivy said, standing very, very still. Suddenly she grabbed his thin little stick of an arm. "I know!" she said. "We'll be tasters."

She was remembering a movie, or maybe a book, she wasn't sure which, but it didn't matter: she had the idea. "From now on, I'll taste your food before you eat it, and you taste mine."

"What if you have nuts?" Ray said. Nuts made Ray sick.

"Like people do for the king," she said, ignoring the question of nuts. "That way we won't get fooled again."

"What king?" Ray asked.

"Oh, Ray," Ivy said. "*Any* king."

He squinted at Ivy and paused. "Don't they get hungry?" he said. "The kings?"

Ivy looked at her brother. There were so many things he just didn't get. "Tasters don't eat *all* the food," she told him. "Just enough to make sure it's not poisoned. So you can eat a bite of mine, and I'll eat a bite of yours."

"What about Dan?" Ray asked.

"Right," Ivy said. "Dan." Actually, Ivy's first thought had been to save herself and Ray. But she liked the idea of saving Dan too. She loved it, actually. And to reward Ray for thinking of it, she declared, "We can *both* taste his food. That way he'll be double protected."

"Carol, too?" Ray asked.

The sad truth about Carol—
which Ivy thought but didn't say—was that it was too
late for her. She'd already *been* poisoned. The best Ivy
could do now was make sure it didn't happen again.
"This is a good plan," she told Ray, reassuringly.
"Trust me." Just saying the words made her feel better,
somehow—lighter. She looked toward the pool then,
and saw Veddy already there, waiting, standing near
the diving board, in full uniform, with a cap—unlike
any lifeguard Ivy had ever seen. *Better* than any lifeguard, she decided. "C'mon," she told Ray. She grabbed
the end of his towel and took off running.

As they approached, Veddy extended his hand
toward the water in the most elegant way, as if he were

offering it to them, and Ray and Ivy, with one quick assenting glance, took flying leaps and cannonballed in.

It was perfect—the crash of their bodies into the water, how the hotness instantly vanished, the way Ivy's head felt like a million bubbles had been released inside it. They pushed off the bottom and came shooting up, human rockets.

"You're it," Ivy said, and Ray instantly closed his eyes and called out, "Marco." Ivy dove and swam to the other side of the pool, emerged, and answered him: "Polo."

 Ray began his blind chase of her voice. In just a few rounds they had changed the game to "Wolf," answered by "Gang," punctuated with growling. And when they got bored with that, they held contests to see who could hold their breath the longest—first sitting on the bottom of the pool, then swimming back and forth across it. Then they took turns acting out scenes under water. One had to guess what the other was doing. "Riding a bike?" "Going fishing?" "Cracking a safe?"

All the while Veddy stood at attention, just far enough back to avoid a single drop on his uniform.

"Dontcha wanna come in?" Ivy called to him.

"Thank you, I prefer higher ground," he said.

"Do you *know* how to swim?" Ray asked.

"Most certainly," he told them, and Ivy thought he sounded a bit offended. "If need be."

After a while Dan came strolling out. He didn't have on his bathing suit, but he walked around the pool, onto the diving board, and straight out to the end of it as if he were going to jump in. He bent down and leaned forward, but at the

last second he reached into
his pocket and tossed out a
handful of change. Nickels,
dimes, quarters, and pennies
rained down into the water and floated to the bottom.
Ray and Ivy dove like porpoises after them, going under
and coming up again until they had collected every
single coin and made leaning silver towers of change
by the side of the pool.

"Finder's keepers," Dan told them, and then, "You
guys look ready for dry land." He pointed out that Ray's
lips were blue.

"That's from his gum," Ivy said, because she didn't
want to get out of the water, and even though she knew
it wasn't really the gum.

"Come on," Dan said, and walked over to one of
the tattered pool chairs. "There's been a change in the
plan."

They hoisted themselves up and over the side and
grabbed their towels. Suddenly the
air felt chilly, and Ivy got goose
bumps. She and Ray chattered
their teeth at each other.

"Carol needs a little time

to recover," Dan started. "So Veddy's going to take her back to the house."

"Now?" Ray said. "Without us?"

"You know what it's like when you're sick," Dan told him. "You just want your own bed and your own pillow."

"She can have mine," Ray offered.

"She just needs a day or two," Dan told him. "Then she and Veddy will catch up with us."

Ivy could feel Ray not liking the plan; she could feel him going in the other direction—back home, with Carol. She didn't want to lose Ray, too. She leaned over and whispered to him, "If poison doesn't kill you, then it clears up pretty fast. She'll be back in no time." She pulled away and looked him in the eye. "Trust me," she said, for the second time that day. She liked the ring of it.

Ivy and Ray followed Dan back toward the motel room, clutching their limp towels around themselves, the sidewalk hot on the bottoms of their bare feet. Carol was waiting for them outside, leaning against the limo. "I'm not going to kiss you," she called out, cupping a hand over her mouth. "Just come give me a little hug goodbye."

She crouched down and they walked into her open arms, and as they did Ivy had a premonition that her mother might whisper some parting words to her. She didn't want her to. Parting words usually entailed something Carol wanted Ivy to do that was practically never any fun. Ivy squeezed her mother hard and quick, but she didn't pull back fast enough.

"Stay on the straight and narrow," Carol whispered—right into Ivy's ear, like a mosquito. Ivy pulled back only in time to see her mother give a quick nod, as if to finalize what she had just said. Then Carol stood up and climbed into the limo, and she and Veddy took off.

The straight and narrow? Where had Ivy heard that before, and what did it mean, anyway? And why did *she* have to do it? What could she say, though? Carol was in the car and away. Dan, Ray, and Ivy stood in the parking lot of the True Vu Motel and waved goodbye.

"Hey," Ray said suddenly, when the car was out of sight, "what'll *we* do? Without the limo?"

Ivy hadn't thought of that, but she quickly said, "I *know*," as if she'd been thinking the exact same thing. And then, dramatically, "Now we're *stranded!*" What a great word, *stranded*—a word she could practically swing on, like a rope over a lake. "We'll languish here," she said. *Languish,* she repeated inside her head. Good words were practically gushing out of her—along with the thrilling prospect of languishing poolside, for days, at the True Vu Motel.

But Dan broke in. "Nope," he said. "No need to languish *or* be stranded. I called Wolfie, and he said he'd come get us in the morning."

"Come get us?" Ray and Ivy said in unison. Wolfgang? Was coming? To *get* them?

SAVING DAN'S LIFE

"Are you sure this is a good idea?" Ivy asked Dan. Wolfgang was due to arrive any minute.

"Sure I'm sure," Dan answered.

Ivy was watching Dan comb his hair in the mirror, admiring the neat, even tracks he made along the side of his head. Ray was over on the unmade bed, bolstered by a mountain of pillows, lost in morning cartoons.

"You'll see," Dan told her. "Wolfie's a stand-up guy."

"Yeah," Ivy said, halfheartedly, unconvinced. She still didn't see what was wrong with staying a few more days at the True Vu Motel, while Carol recovered. Hadn't they had a great time last night? Ivy had put her doubts and suspicions behind her—forgot about poison and the inky-haired waitress and staying on the straight and narrow and whatever awaited them at Wolfgang's. She and Ray had gone swimming again, and Dan ordered in pizza for dinner. Then they walked down the road to a dairy bar and had soft-serve dipped in chocolate. Back at the motel they all stayed up late watching a movie on TV about a jewel robbery. Ivy had learned the word *heist*.

But now, in the blasting sunlight of morning, there was no denying that Carol was gone—she was home, poisoned—and Wolfie was coming to get them. Everything seemed highly suspect to Ivy once again—and *not*, she reminded herself, because anyone was a werewolf.

"Where does Wolfgang live?" Ivy asked.

"Pennsylvania," Dan said. "Where *pencils* are made."

"What did he *do*?" Ivy wanted to know.

"Do?" Dan repeated.

"To get in jail."

"Counterfeit," Dan said. "One of the greats."

Ivy repeated *counterfeit* inside her head. It was a good word, no two ways about it, solid as a stick. "Counterfeit what?" she said. She had it in her mind that counterfeit meant money, but she wasn't entirely sure.

"Documents," Dan told her. "A wide range of things."

"Can *anything* be counterfeit?" she asked.

"Just about," he said, flashing that quick grin of his. "All that glitters is not gold," he reminded her. He retrieved his money clip from the top of the dresser and announced he was going to settle up with the man in the office. "Stay outta trouble," he said, brushing his hand over the top of her head as he walked to the door.

Ivy joined Ray on the unmade bed. He was watching a commercial.

"I wish Carol was here," he said, eyes still on the screen.

"Yeah," Ivy agreed. She kept expecting Carol to walk out of the bathroom and ask her and Ray if they wanted cereal, or tell them to pick up their clothes off the floor, or remind them that she hadn't even had her first cup of coffee.

The cartoon came back on. Wile E. Coyote was in a rowboat, surrounded by sharks.

Ivy had seen a show on TV, once, about a man who had his arm eaten by a shark. He said that for a long time after his arm was gone, he still felt like he had it.

He even had a name for it. "Carol's our phantom limb," Ivy said, dramatically.

Ray turned away from the cartoon. "What?" he said.

"Our phantom limb," she repeated. She took great pleasure saying the words. "Like when a shark eats your arm but you think you still have it."

Ray's eyes got big and he didn't say anything. He just looked at Ivy.

"It's real," she told him. "It happens. I saw it on TV."

"Why?" he asked.

"Why? Why what?"

"Why do you think you still have your arm?"

Ivy sighed. Sometimes Ray just didn't get it. "Because I *do*," she told him, flapping her hand near his face. "I'm just talking about what it *feels* like without Carol."

"Oh," he said, turning back to the TV. "Yeah."

Ivy watched Ray watch cartoons for a little while. His face killed her. "She'll be back," Ivy said. "Carol." Carol always came back. She came back from jail, she came back after she and Dan had fights. "She's not gonna let a little poison ruin our summer vacation!" Ivy promised.

Suddenly the doorknob rattled and Dan stuck his head into the room. "Wolfie's here. Saddle up," he told them. "Wolfie's not a Mann you keep waiting."

Ray and Ivy hopped off the bed and started grabbing whatever clothes were still strewn around. They stuffed everything into their suitcases and snapped them shut. That's when Ivy heard it—the ticking. She grabbed Ray's shoulder and they both stood at attention, listening. No doubt about it: a definite ticking sound, just outside their room. With Ivy in the lead, they tiptoed forward to investigate and through the crack in the door spotted a slightly vibrating, boxy-looking car the color of bronze gold. There was Dan, standing beside it, and next to him an elflike man with a wild gray beard. *That* was Wolfie? Suspected were-wolf, big bad influence, the man who couldn't be kept waiting? He was old! He was wearing a dirty apron over his clothes! He had holes in his shoes!

"D'you see his *hands*?" Ray whispered.

Ivy nodded. Wolfie's hands were huge. "But not hairy," she pointed out. She wanted to keep a lid on any werewolf worries. She had the car to think about. Why was it *ticking*?

Dan spotted Ray and Ivy and motioned them outside. "Meet Wolfie," he said as they stepped through the door. "Wolfgang Mann."

Wolfgang leaned forward and zoomed right in on them. "Yaah?" he said. "So these are your *schätzles*? You ready to go? Come mit me, ve got *verk* to do!" And he trotted around to the back of his car and opened up the trunk. Ivy thought he moved awfully fast for an old person. For a second she even wondered if he was really a young person just dressed up to *look* old. "Load the buggy up," he told them, and they handed over their bags.

A moment later they were settled in the back seat of the ticking, vibrating gold car.

"Off ve go," Wolfie announced from the driver's seat. "To the castle!"

Castle?

He peeled out of the True Vu parking lot and took off so fast that Ivy and Ray lost their stomachs on the first hill. Stretching as tall as he could in the driver's

seat, Wolfie looked at them in the rearview mirror and
laughed. "You like roller coasters?" he asked. The back of
his head was freckled above his ring of white hair. They
hadn't even answered him before he asked something
else: "You gonna help me mit the job for your papa?"

It took Ray and Ivy a moment to connect "papa" with
Dan, and when they did it made them laugh.

"What job?" Ray asked.

Counterfeit, Ivy assumed.

"Box making," Dan answered. He turned around
in his seat. "Wolfie here is a master craftsman. I asked
him to make up a presentation box for the Mouton
family heirloom. Presentation's half the game, you
know."

"What game?" Ray asked.

"The game of life!" Dan declared. "The only game in town."

Wolfie slammed on the brakes.

"*Eine schildkröte*," he announced, opening his door and springing out of the car. Just a moment later he was back with a beautiful tortoise cupped in his wide, farmer's hand. "Vant to see?" he said, holding it at eye level in front of Ray and Ivy. "She's a beauty, yaah?"

The turtle had a gorgeous shell, dark and diamonded, its rim a waxy yellow, the color of a bruise Ivy'd had, once, after a boy named Scot punched her arm. The turtle's head was drawn in, but his legs were pedaling madly, still working at a getaway.

"Vhat you think? Should ve take him home and make *schildkröte* soup?"

Ivy and Ray gasped in unison, horrified.

Wolfie laughed. "OK, you don't vant soup, no soup. Maybe ve should put him vhere he belongs? Come mit me."

"I'll pull the car over," Dan said. He winked at Ray

and Ivy as they hopped out to follow Wolfie across the
street. There, a sharp slope led into tangled woods—
Hansel and Gretel woods, Ivy thought. Before she
knew it, Wolfie was tearing down the hill, holding out
the turtle ahead of him, and Ray was right behind.
What could she do but follow? At the bottom, Wolfie
squatted down and lowered the turtle onto the ground.
Ray squatted next to him. Ivy held back and watched
them all—Wolfie, Ray, the turtle.

Wolfie placed his big hand across the shell and gave a little pat. "OK, fella," he said. "Time to go."

Ray solemnly nodded. "Bye."

They all observed in silence as the creature began his slow procession into the woods. "Don't play in traffic," Ivy called out suddenly—something Dan sometimes said. It seemed appropriate, given the circumstances.

They watched until the turtle's getaway was secure, and then Wolfie straightened up and brushed his hands together. "No *schildkrötensuppe* for us," he said with a sigh.

Suddenly Ivy saw plain as day that Wolfie had never for one second planned to put the turtle in a soup. She'd been gullible, she realized, and that panged her. The next time Wolfie teased, she wouldn't fall for it.

They began their climb back up the slope.

"Hey, look vhat's here!" Wolfie said.

All Ray and Ivy saw was a tangle of earth and leaves and roots. But Wolfie was squatting low again, digging as if for hidden treasure. Suddenly he held up his prize. A mushroom! Ivy recognized it, though it didn't look anything like the mushrooms she saw in the store, all white and clean, stacked like little soldiers under the plastic wrap. Wolfie's mushroom had a lopsided crown and a crooked stem, and it was dirty. "C'mon!" he said, already back at work, digging for more.

The mushrooms were right under their noses, but it took Ivy and Ray a while to spot them. Eventually, though, they began to find what they were looking for—one mushroom, and then another, and another.

Wolfie inspected each mushroom before adding it to the sling he had made with his apron. "Hey, ve're making out like bandits!" he said, jostling the harvest they had gathered. "Let's go show your papa."

They found Dan leaning against the gold car, face raised up to the sun, catching some rays. "Your *schätzles* got good eyes," Wolfie called out, and though Ivy didn't know what *schätzle* meant, she suspected it was a compliment, and she never minded being paid one. Plus she felt the particular satisfaction of having unearthed buried treasure. It wasn't until they had roared off in the ticking car once again and speeded up over the crest of a hill that Ivy became suspicious about just what Wolfie planned to *do* with the mushrooms.

For nearly an hour Wolfie zoomed along back roads that were anything but straight and narrow. Dan fell asleep in the front seat with his head tilted to the side and his mouth dropped open. Normally Ivy and Ray would have imitated him and added loud, honking, snoring noises, too, but Ivy had bigger things—poison and counterfeit among them—to think about.

Finally Wolfie brought them onto the main street of a small town. They passed by a run-down little restaurant called the Pancake and Omelet Factory, and Ray elbowed Ivy and gave it the thumbs-up sign. So Ray was thinking about food, Ivy realized, while she was busy thinking how to keep them all alive, not to mention on the straight and narrow. In many ways, it seemed to Ivy, Ray had a much easier time of it than she did.

Now they were chugging up a hill lined with small, boxy houses on either side. Battered trashcans stood guard at the bottom of short, cracked-pavement driveways. Ivy wanted to believe they were on their way to a castle, even though it didn't look like a castle kind of neighborhood. She didn't want to be gullible again, as she'd been about the turtle. And maybe the mushrooms!

Suddenly Wolfie made a quick left and pulled up to a small, squat brick house. It reminded Ivy of the third little pig's home that wouldn't blow down. It was definitely *not* a castle.

"I *knew* it wouldn't be," Ivy whispered to Ray, just for the record.

Ray was wide-eyed, though, ready for anything.

"Come mit me," Wolfie told them, springing out of the car. "I'll give you the royal tour."

He led them in through a side door. "My verkshop," he announced.

"Nice setup," Dan said, nodding approvingly.

It had once been a plain old garage—Ivy could see that easily enough—but now it was something else altogether, filled to the brim with machines and contraptions, outfitted with heavy black presses with handles like the steering wheels of ships, and a cutting machine with a giant blade as long as Ray was tall, and workbenches and stools and tools and braids of twine and wooden boards, and papers and stamps and weights. It was obviously a place where things were *made*.

Ray's nose was twitching. The verkshop smelled

like cigars—so had Wolfie's car—but with leather and ink mixed in, too. It was the smell, Ivy thought, of concoctions.

Wolfie walked over to the workbench and picked up a small red leather box. "All ready for your ruby," he told them, and flipped it open to reveal scarlet velvet padding. "Now," Wolfie said, turning to Dan, "time for the die."

Ivy grabbed Ray's shoulder and froze. Had Wolfie said *die*?

Dan didn't miss a beat, though—just reached into his pocket, nice and easy, and extracted a block of metal the size of a small picture frame.

Ivy loosened her grip on Ray, but she remained wary as she leaned in for a closer look. "What *is* it?" she asked.

"This, my chickadees, is the Mouton family crest!" Dan told them.

The face of the block was filled with lines and squiggles; Ivy made out the shape of a shield, with a triangle in the middle.

"Lotta history in that baby," Dan said. "All part of the story. That band across the top contains the family motto—in *Latin*, no less," he told them.

Ivy and Ray looked even closer. It was hard to believe that actual words could fit in such a tiny space. Ivy thought of a necklace she'd coveted once, in a gift shop, that had the whole Lord's Prayer written on it in words tiny as a pinhead. "What's it say?" she asked.

"He who wishes the kernel must crack the nut."

Ivy remembered what Carol had said about their family tree being a nut tree.

"I want to remind Gladys that we go back a long way," Dan told them.

Wolfie took the block from Dan and secured it inside a brass holder mounted on a machine at the end of the workbench. He clicked the contraption on. "Once the die gets good and varm," he told them, "ve gonna shtamp it in gold on the box." He led them out of the workshop then, and Ivy felt compelled to whisper to Ray, "Die's the *real* name for it, that's all."

Wolfie showed them the kitchen and living room, the bath and bedrooms. Except for the workshop it was a very ordinary house, filled with things that didn't strike Ivy as the least bit suspicious. Every room was square and solid and neat. After all the grandness of Marietta's big house, there was something about how snug Wolfie's place was that felt good to Ivy, almost irresistible. But it *wasn't* a castle, she reminded herself, just to keep the record straight.

"You two *schätzles* are gonna share this room," Wolfie said, showing them their bedroom.

Ray beamed at the prospect. Ivy was glad, too, though she didn't want to show it. Instead she gave a thumbs-up to the fat, puffy comforters that Wolfie called featherbeds. She looked forward to jumping on clouds, Ray and her.

But then Wolfie announced, "Now ve eat and then ve verk—how's that sound?"

It didn't sound good—at least to Ivy. She remembered the dirty, crooked mushrooms. And Carol throwing up in the bushes. The inky-haired waitress. What if Wolfie was out to get them?

As she and Ray followed Wolfie and Dan back to the kitchen, she tapped Ray on the shoulder and made big eyes at him. "What?" Ray blurted out, but Ivy made even bigger eyes and he hushed. Then she put her hands around her throat and stuck her tongue out like she was dying, but all Ray did was laugh. By then they were back in the kitchen, at the chunky wooden table with painted chairs, and Wolfie was telling them to pull up a seat. Each place was already set with a little wooden board, a knife, and a cloth napkin.

Wolfie went right to work at the sink, cleaning each of the mushrooms with a small brush with a knob on it. He had them chopped up and sizzling in a pan of butter in no time. He brought out big, thick sausages that looked like swollen hot dogs and then scooped out a dish of sauerkraut from a barrel over in the corner. He put a jar of dark, grainy mustard on the table, along with a couple of hunks of cheese and a whole loaf of dark bread.

"Vhat?" he said when he saw Ray and Ivy eyeing the food skeptically. Ray would rather have been looking at a grilled cheese sandwich and potato chips; Ivy's concerns were far more grave.

"Just like in the old country!" Wolfie said, encouraging them to begin.

From the corner of her eye Ivy watched as Dan, seated to her left, reached for his fork and lifted a big bite of seasoned, simmered, shrunken brown mushrooms to his mouth.

"Stop!" she shrieked, thrusting out her hand toward him as if officially ordering the mushrooms to halt. And they did. Everything and everyone froze.

"Is there a problem?" Dan said.

"I want to taste them," she said. "First." She did

not want to taste them first—or *ever*! Why were those words coming out of her mouth?

She looked across the table to Ray, miserably. He finally understood what was on her mind, and it showed all over his pale, wide-eyed face. He swallowed hard and said in a small voice, "Me, too." Full of dread though she was, Ivy couldn't help but smile at Ray. What a good brother, with her to the very end.

Dan shrugged. "Be my guest. By all means," he said, and set his fork back down. He nodded to Wolfie and told him, "Never knew my kids had such a hankering for mushrooms."

The time had come. Ray and Ivy slowly lifted their forks, raising them off their napkins as if invisible chains were holding them in place, lowering them to the small mound of mushrooms before them as if descending into quicksand. They both let their forks muddle around in the mushrooms for a while, sliding as many as they could away from the prongs of their forks, searching for the smallest single bit they could spear. Once again they exchanged looks—deadly serious looks. And then, in silent communication, as if they were counting *One, two, three, go,* the way they always started their races with each other, Ray and

Ivy simultaneously lifted their forks to their mouths and popped in their bites. Neither chewed. There was a second's pause—mushroom in mouth, eyes wide, *goodbye*—and then they swallowed. They both reached for the glasses of milk Wolfie had poured them and gulped down as much as they could. Ivy's heart was pounding so hard she couldn't tell if she was dying or not. She studied Ray. He looked OK. So far.

"Ha!" Wolfie said. "You think they vill kill you, these *pilze*?" And then he dug into his own serving of mushrooms with gusto. Ivy watched in stunned silence and wondered why she hadn't thought

to let Wolfie go first to begin with. She and Ray had risked their lives for nothing!

By this time Dan had started in too. Ivy held her breath. She continued to watch Ray intently, looking for any danger signs. But she saw no evidence of twitching, no gagging or drooling. Nothing. Just that good face of his. Same with Dan, right next to her, shoveling in the sausage and sauerkraut and mushrooms. Wolfie was cleaning his plate. If there was poison, Ivy finally concluded, they were *all* goners.

But when minute after minute passed and nothing happened, Ivy realized with a spreading embarrassment that she might have jumped to conclusions about Wolfie being a poisoner. People weren't dropping like flies, she noted. So she let Wolfie cut her slices of bread, and she and Ray used the silver scraper with the slit in it to peel off thin strips of cheese. The mustard was hot and spicy. Ivy liked the cheese and eating off the little wooden board instead of a plate, and Ray liked the sausage, and they both liked the bread. Neither tried the sauerkraut. Or any more of the mushrooms. They had done their duty as far as the mushrooms were concerned.

FINE DISTINCTIONS

After lunch, Wolfie said it was time to have a shmoke and check out the estate.

"We don't shmoke," Ivy told him.

Wolfie nodded. "All right, then," he said. "I'll meet you in a few minutes and ve'll make vhat needs to be made—how's that sound?"

Dan proclaimed it a perfect afternoon for the pursuit of knowledge and a nap. He grabbed his book—*Strike It Rich Through Self-Publishing*—and made his way out to a lawn chair beneath the apple tree in Wolfie's back yard.

No sooner were Dan and Wolfie out the door than Ivy called a meeting.

"Where?" Ray asked.

"Featherbeds," she answered. They needed privacy, and she wanted to try out the jumping. She also wanted to revise her theory about poisoning before Ray could accuse her of having jumped to conclusions.

They made a beeline to their bedroom. Ivy walked over to her bed and flung herself backwards onto the mound of comforter. It was wonderfully soft and produced a satisfying *whoosh* as she threw her weight against it. Ray did the same on his. Then they pushed the beds closer together and spread the comforter over the space between them to make a blanket roof. They crawled inside, and Ivy called the meeting to order.

"When do you think Carol will come?" Ray began. His agenda was often different from Ivy's.

But his question led neatly to the new theory she'd just come up with. "Carol's faking," Ivy told him.

"Faking?"

"Definitely," Ivy said. "There's no poison." Hadn't he learned anything from the mushrooms?

"But why would she *fake*?" Ray asked.

Didn't Ray suspect anyone of anything, ever? "People do," she said. "They fake all the time. *You* do," she reminded him. "To get out of school."

"So do you," he said.

"So you see my point," Ivy finished.

"But why *would* she?" Ray asked again. "We're on vacation."

Ivy sighed. She felt that she knew a great deal more than Ray about their parents. (Actually, she felt that she knew a great deal more than he did about *everything*.) "She doesn't want to be part of Dan's plan to get the fortune," she told him. "She's through being an accomplice." Being his accomplice was what had sent her to prison last time. "She's gone straight," Ivy said. She pictured her mother's serious, uncurled hair, pointing down to her shoulders, flat and even all the way around. As if she had ironed it. "She definitely won't be showing up here at Wolfie's."

"Why not?" Ray asked.

"I told you. She thinks Wolfie is a bad influence. She doesn't want him to rub off on Dan."

"Rub off?"

"That's what bad influences do: they rub off on other people. Like a crumbly eraser."

Ray got quiet. A few moments later he said, almost defiantly, "I *like* Wolfie."

"Yeah," Ivy said. "I know. But you like *everyone*, pretty much." She said it as gently as she could. "We still need to keep our eyes peeled. For danger signs," she told him. "Get the list."

Ray dutifully crawled out of the fort and retrieved their notebook from his suitcase. As soon as she had it in hand, Ivy started writing additions: *Turtl Soop. Mushrooms.* And last but not least: *Die.*

"Why are *they* danger signs?" Ray asked.

"Because—" Ivy began, and then stopped. The real answer was that they had scared her, but she didn't want to say so.

"None of them turned out bad," Ray said.

"I *know* that," Ivy answered. "But they *could* have. Plus what's with all this *castle* stuff? And tours of the *estate*. What's he talking about?"

"That's just the way he talks. It's his whatchama-callit—his accent."

"No," Ivy declared. "His accent is *verkshop*. And *shmoke*. Not *castle*."

"It *could* be," Ray tried.

"No, it couldn't," Ivy said, but she wasn't going to pursue it. She had other points to make. "Why's he being so nice to us? Why did he come and pick us up at the motel? Why's he shtamping the family crest on a box for the ruby?"

"Because he's nice?" Ray suggested.

Ivy sighed. "Oh, Ray," she said, just a sliver away from contempt. "There's got to be more to it than that. Haven't you ever heard of *counterfeit*?" And even though she had learned about counterfeit only that morning, once Ivy learned something she felt that she had always known it—and that it was up to her to share her knowl-edge. "Counterfeit is when you make a fake copy of something that's real. Like money. Fake money."

"Monopoly," Ray said.

"Well, yeah," Ivy agreed. "Only it looks so real that

people *fall* for it. You couldn't really spend Monopoly money."

"Does *Wolfie* make money in his verkshop?" Ray asked suddenly. The notion was clearly a jolt to his system, and he sat up so straight his head touched their featherbed roof, which was beginning to sag.

"Not that I know of," Ivy had to admit. "But you can counterfeit anything, you know. Maybe they're planning to make a counterfeit of the Mouton family ruby! And maybe Carol is afraid Dan'll be caught and sent up the river again—and our family will be torn asunder!" She warmed to the sound of her voice and her grown-up words as the story drew to its tragic conclusion in her mind.

"Under what?" Ray said.

Ivy looked at him. It took her a moment to figure out his question. Then she said, "Under nothing. *Asunder.*" She'd learned the word from a book about the Civil War. "Split up," she explained. "On different sides of the fence."

"What fence?"

"*Any* fence, Ray."

"Oh," Ray said. "Do you think Carol will come *tomorrow*?"

Just then there was a knock on their door. "Hey, you two," Wolfie called. "What are ve—shlackers? It's time to do some verk!"

Ray and Ivy crawled out from underneath the featherbed fort, and Ivy stuffed their list back in the suitcase. Then they followed Wolfie into his shop. He led them to the workbench that ran the length of the wall and pulled out two stools, one on either side of the stamping machine. "Hop up on your thrones," he told them.

Ivy rolled her eyes; Ray claimed his seat.

The family crest had heated up. Wolfie gave it a quick feel with the tip of his index finger and declared it just the right temperature. He positioned the leather-bound box beneath the die and covered it with a piece of gold cellophane. Then he let Ivy and Ray bring down the handle that lowered the metal die onto the gold and the top of the box. They gave it a little squeeze and then released it.

"Ready?" Wolfie asked, and peeled back the gold cellophane to reveal a beautiful stamped impression, shiny and crisp, embedded in the top of the box. Ray and Ivy leaned in close to inspect the little ribbon of Latin words waving out across the red leather. It was all

very fancy, and so classy that Ivy had a pang of missing Carol. Wolfie rubbed a piece of cloth over the stamping, and it shone even brighter.

"Is it *real* gold?" Ray asked.

Ivy gave a heavy click of her tongue. Hadn't he ever heard "All that glitters is not gold"? "If that was real gold," she said, "it'd be worth—" but before she could decide between billions and bezillions, Wolfie jumped in.

"Gold *foil*," he said. "Genuine gold foil."

"It *is*?" Ivy found it hard to believe. "Genuine?"

"You bet," Wolfie said.

She gave the stamped box an even closer inspection. Was she looking at the real thing?

"Same as your ruby," Wolfie told them. "Genuine."

Ivy's eyes narrowed. "How do you *know*?"

Wolfie waggled his pointer finger at her. "About these things, I *know*. I'm an expert!"

Ivy took his words to heart. She deferred to experts. (She considered *herself* an expert in any number of areas.) Wolfie might be a counterfeiter, she reasoned, but who would know better than a counterfeiter what was genuine and what wasn't?

That night, Wolfie turned in early—"mit the birdies," he said—and Dan and Ivy and Ray watched the ballgame on TV. Every once in a while they could hear Wolfie snoring in the other room.

"Shnoring," Ivy said.

"Shleeping," Ray responded.

The game went into extra innings, but Dan let them stay up and the Red Sox finally won.

It was close to midnight when Ray and Ivy stumbled off the couch and into the bathroom to get ready for bed. And they were standing at the sink together, reaching for their toothbrushes, when they saw them—Wolfie's choppers, his teeth, a mouthful of them, right there on display in the dish next to the soap.

They froze. They'd never seen false teeth before. Ivy half expected the teeth to chatter. Or smile. Or do something. She honestly thought she saw them move, just a bit. She and Ray dared each other to touch them. Ivy went first. She cautiously raised her finger and touched a top molar, then drew back her hand as if

she'd been burned. Ray did the same. Then they fled, unbrushed, unwashed, thrilled.

They tore into the bedroom and dove onto their featherbeds as if skeletons were chasing them. A moment later, though, Ivy was back up, scavenging for their notepad in Ray's suitcase. She plunked down next to Ray on his bed and turned to a fresh blank page.

"New danger signs?" Ray said.

"New *list*," Ivy informed him. She made two columns on the page, one titled *Real* and the other *Fake*. "That's what it all boils down to," she told him. Under *Fake*, she wrote *teeth*. Then she added *poison*. Below *Real* she listed *gold* and *ruby*.

"I thought Wolfie said they were *genuine*," Ray quibbled.

"Lights out," Dan ordered, appearing suddenly in their doorway. He motioned to Ivy to get back into her own bed.

"Is genuine the same as real?" Ray asked him.

"Ah, a fine distinction," he answered, flashing that quick grin of his. "Not exactly the same, but related." He kissed them both and switched out the light.

They lay in the dark, quiet for a while.

Then Ray asked, "Is real always better?"

"Better than fake," Ivy told him. "And real's *worth* more."

"But you can't help it," Ray said, "if you need fake teeth."

That was true. "I didn't say fake was *bad*," she told him. "Just not real. These are *fine* distinctions we're making."

They got quiet again.

"Ivy?" Ray said, a minute later.

"What?"

"Do you still think Wolfie is counterfeit?"

"No," she said. She really didn't. And she could tell Ray was relieved, even in the dark.

"He's gone straight," Ray said contentedly. "Like Carol."

Ivy paused. "Right," she said. Then she promised him, "She'll meet up with us soon."

Once again they stopped talking, settled deeper into their beds.

Suddenly Ivy sprang up. "Dentures!" she sang out.

Ray startled. "What?"

"That's the *real* word for them," Ivy said. "For fake teeth." She was glad it had come to her. She liked knowing—and saying—what something really was.

RIDING HIGH

Ivy awoke the next morning with her neck a little stiff and a spot of drool on the front of her nightgown. She stretched herself up to full sitting position and looked around.

"Where are we?" she asked. They weren't at Wolfie's. They were on the road. Dan was sailing along.

"Took a little detour," he said, smiling at her in the rearview mirror. "Thought I'd surprise you."

A detour from where? she wondered. *To* where? *No*where? Ivy looked out the window at the straight, empty road ahead of them. They were surrounded by flat fields. Here a barn, there a house, field, field, barn. "Is this Florida?" she asked.

"Nope," Dan said. "Won't make Florida for a while. But we're on our way."

Now Ray was waking up, stirring out of his balled-up shape, blinking, rubbing his eyes. The first thing he said when he sat up was "Wow!"

Ivy turned to see what he could possibly be looking

at, and there, in the distance, where *nothing* had been before, loomed, in the fragile early-morning light—a roller coaster! It was old and wooden, and zigzagged across the sky. Ivy could hardly believe she was seeing it. "Where *are* we?" she asked again.

"Pen-cil Vania," Dan answered in his best Count Dracula voice. "Hershey, to be exact. Chocolate World."

"Can we go on it?" Ray said. His gaze hadn't budged from the roller coaster.

"What else would we *do*," Dan said, "but go on it?"

Ivy's heart soared. The day dawned in front of her like a present just waiting to be opened.

"Just be sure and tell Carol we made an educational stop on our journey."

Ray and Ivy recoiled. *Educational?*

"Hershey, Pennsylvania, is a gold mine of family history," Dan said.

Ivy's heart hiccupped. Family history? Was there no getting away from it? She saw their day going up in smoke, scorched by boring facts and research. She checked to make sure the roller coaster was still up ahead, looming. Maybe it was a mirage. Ivy had seen some desert movies; she knew about those shimmering pools that disappeared when the wanderers—dying of thirst and burnt to a crisp—finally got to them.

"Milton Hershey and Blackstone Mouton were from the same generation of millionaires," Dan continued. "But they did entirely different things with their money. Hershey made a fortune making chocolate—and then built the town of his dreams with it."

"What about the roller coaster?" Ray asked.

"Town of his dreams?" Ivy repeated.

"Created his own little utopia," Dan told them. "Know what that is?"

Ivy thought the word—*utopia*—sounded like something you could eat.

"It's a place built on an idea," Dan said. "A philosophy about how life should be lived. Hershey set things up just the way he wanted them."

The notion instantly appealed to Ivy, especially the part about setting things up just the way you wanted.

"What about the roller coaster?" Ray asked again, obviously trying to get Dan back on track.

"Our first stop after breakfast," Dan promised, and when Mama's Coffee Shop appeared at the next crossroads, a blue and white OPEN flag billowing from its corner, Dan pulled in without even calling for a vote.

"Is Carol meeting us *here*?" Ray asked.

Ivy almost laughed at his question but stopped herself. They were, after all, back on the road, at a place called Chocolate World, and a roller coaster had just magically appeared out of nowhere. Clearly, anything could happen.

"Not quite yet," Dan said. "But soon."

Ray and Ivy pulled on pants and shirts right over their pj's, found their flip-flops, and scrambled after Dan into Mama's. A bunch of barrel-chested men sat at the counter, but there were three free stools at the

end and Ray and Ivy made a beeline for them. Twirling seats were better than a booth, and since Carol wasn't with them, this was their chance.

The miniature boxes of cereal on the shelf over the grill instantly caught Ray's eye, and when the waitress came to take their orders that was what he chose—Frosted Flakes. Ivy felt the tug of the little boxes, too, but stuck with her old standby, French toast, and Dan ordered tons: eggs, potatoes, sausage, hash, coffee, juice. Ivy watched the waitress's pencil flying across her little green pad and admired how she got it all down. "Drinks for you two?" she asked Ivy and Ray.

While they waited for food to come, Dan went to wash up and Ivy and Ray spun on their seats, pacing their rotations to avoid total knee collision. They twirled in perfect sync and increased their speed with each revolution, round after round. Dizziness crept up on Ivy slowly and then overtook her entirely. "Hey," she cried out, suddenly, braking herself at the counter with both hands. Ray kept right on going around. Ivy's head was spinning from more than the twirling. For one thing, their dreamlike departure had come back to her: Dan lifting them out of their beds in the middle of the night, loading all their stuff into Wolfie's car.

"How come we left?" she asked—of no one in particular. Then she extended her arm and stopped Ray cold, right in mid-twirl. "What about *Wolfie?*" she said. "Does he *know* we left?" In a smaller, quieter voice she almost squeaked, "Does he know we took his *car?*"

Ray only looked at her, big eyes, didn't say a word.

"This could be trouble," Ivy said. She feared a serious lapse in judgment or behavior, or both, on Dan's part. Words cascaded inside her head. Robbery. *Highway* robbery! She stole a quick glance out the window, at the country road beyond. It wasn't a highway, she reassured herself. But other words kept coming. Larceny. *Grand* larceny! Felony!—words she didn't even know she knew.

"Do you think we hurt Wolfie's feelings?" Ray said.

Ivy studied her brother. His way of thinking never ceased to amaze her. Here she was, trying to keep them all alive, on the straight and narrow, out of jail, and there was Ray, worried about hurt feelings! She gave him a push with her hand that sent him revolving again.

Dan was on his way back to the counter. One look at Ivy's face and he instantly suspected something. "What?" he said.

"What what?" Ivy answered, as innocent as she could be.

He studied her. "Something on your mind?" he asked.

She shook her head no, pinched her lips together, gave what she hoped was a nonchalant shrug. "We were just saying what a stand-up guy Wolfie is ..." She brushed an imaginary crumb off the counter.

Dan nodded.

"... and how it's too bad we didn't get to say goodbye," she said, sad but sweet.

"I couldn't sleep, didn't see any reason to dawdle," Dan said. "Gladys isn't getting any younger, you know." He took a sip of his coffee. It was so hot it made him squint when he swallowed.

"But he *knew* we were going," Ivy said, trying not to make it a question. "In *his* car."

Dan laughed and put his coffee cup back on the circle of the saucer. "What, you think I'd pull a fast one on Wolfie? Make off with his car? You have a suspicious nature, Ivy girl," he said.

"Jumps to conclusions," Ray piped in as he completed yet another revolution.

"Of course he knows!" Dan said, leaning in close to her. "He *offered* us his car. Like I told you—and you told me—Wolfie's a stand-up guy."

Relief flowed through Ivy, loosened her joints, let her exhale. It even eased the sting of having been wrong. "I know," she said. "I knew that." Leaning in even closer to Dan, she whispered, "Ray was just worried we hurt Wolfie's feelings."

It was still early and the massive parking lot at Chocolate World was nearly empty when they pulled in after breakfast. Ray and Ivy hopped out of the car into a day that was already keeping its promise to get hot. Ivy realized she still had on her pj's under her clothes, but she didn't say anything. She liked feeling ready for day or night, all in one.

Dan let out a low whistle of admiration. He was leaning up against the car, studying the looping landscape of roller-coaster tracks before them. "Now *that's* a piece of work," he said. "When ole Hershey built this town it was one of the first things he brought in. Wanted his workers to have a little fun."

Ivy and Ray studied the zigzaggy path of empty tracks. "The roller coaster was a *present*?" she said.

"*Good* present," Ray said solemnly, and then he and Ivy headed off, straight toward the entrance to the park. They hadn't gone far, though, before they stopped. "Closed," Ray called back to Dan, his little hands rising up by his sides.

Ivy pointed out the posted hours.

Dan never broke his loose, long-legged stride up to the gates. "Those are the *official* hours," he said, as if anything official had nothing to do with them.

A young woman dressed in a long skirt and a frilly shirt—olden-days costume, Ivy thought—explained to Dan through the bars that the park was not open to the general public until ten o'clock.

Dan turned to Ivy and smiled. "General public," he said—another thing, like *official*, that clearly didn't refer to them. He turned back to the fresh-faced woman behind the gates. "No problem," he told her, "we're just scouting. For the movie."

Ivy was suddenly all ears. Dan could always uncork a good story when he needed to.

A slight blush rose in the young woman's face. "Movie?" she asked.

Dan paused, seemed a bit surprised. "So the higher-ups haven't put out the word yet?" he said. "Not to worry. They're probably keeping the news under wraps till we have a definite shooting schedule and all the actors in place."

"Shooting schedule?"

"For the movie. Right now we're still in the research stage." He leaned in a bit toward her. "There's a major book deal in the works. Foreign rights, talk shows—not to mention the movie. The whole nine yards. It's in the early stages, of course, but we're here, on location,

to see what—and who—might have a place in the film." He took a step back and held up his hands to frame what he saw before him: the woman's slightly confused face, the roller coaster as scenery behind her. 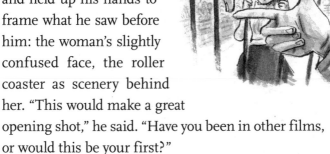"This would make a great opening shot," he said. "Have you been in other films, or would this be your first?"

The woman smiled—a tentative, nervous smile.

Ivy could feel her wavering about whether to open the gates to them or not. "It's just that only guests of the hotel are allowed in before ten. And actually," she apologized, "it's a little early even for *them* to get in!" She dutifully recited the rules but was clearly aching to relax them.

"Guests of the hotel!" Dan said brightly, as if everything had fallen into place. He lifted his arms to the sky. "Well, that settles it!"

The woman paused as if she might ask something more, but then she didn't. She turned the key and pressed down on the gold handle and pulled back the heavy iron gate. Dan flashed his million-dollar smile as he, Ray, and Ivy slipped inside.

"What hotel?" Ray called to Ivy as they broke into a run toward the roller coaster. "What book?"

"The *official* ones," Ivy said. He was *so* gullible!

Not one but *two* roller coasters awaited Ivy and Ray! Dueling roller coasters, they were called, built right next to each other, with parallel tracks and turns and dives. It was almost too good to be true, Ivy thought— as if Mr. Hershey had built one for her and one for Ray, so they could race. And they had them both all to themselves. The ride operator said he wasn't really open for business yet, but after a whispered conversation with Dan he told them to climb aboard anyway and he'd give them an early-bird special. Of course Ivy took the lead car in one and Ray the lead car in the other. Dan declined each of their invitations to come along. He said that breakfast was too recent a memory and he'd be of more use on the sidelines, ready to declare the winner in the case of a photo finish. "May the best kid win," he called out, waving, as the operator yanked back the handle and the two trains of box seats started clicking and rattling up the first big climb.

Ivy gripped the handle and looked straight ahead. Up, and up, and up, methodically and mechanically notching along, all the metal pieces knocking and locking and grabbing the seats onward and upward. Higher, higher. Ivy gripped the silver bar tighter, every muscle in her body tensed, alert. And then, in the remaining seconds before she reached the very top of the first hill, the point of no return, Ivy got them: second thoughts. They hit her like an avalanche. Going on this roller coaster was *crazy*! She didn't *want* to, she'd *never* wanted to. Why did they *make* her? How did the cars stay on the rails anyway? What if she died? What if Ray won?

She could see the very top now, the big drop-off, the place beyond which she could see nothing more of the track she was on, as if she were about to sail off into thin air. Oh, why hadn't she and Ray at least gone together? Ray! In the final nanosecond before she went over the crest, Ivy turned to see her brother—one last look. And there he was, *even* with her, across from her on his own track, in his own car at the head of his own roller coaster, clutching the silver bar in front of him, hair blowing, mouth wide open. Their eyes met, their cars tipped past the peak, and together, in perfect har-

mony, they let it rip, screaming their hearts out—huge, trailing, cascading screams that surrounded them all the way down and around and up the next hill and into the turn, around and down again, up, down. Once they took off there was no stopping, no time, no second thoughts, no thoughts at all, just the ride, right until the final moment when their cars jolted to a halt and it was over.

Ivy opened her eyes, turned her head. There was Ray again, looking at her. They were alive! And here came Dan, striding out toward them, nodding approval.

"Who won?" she called out.

"Can we go again?" Ray asked.

"It was a dead heat," Dan told them. "You sure you're ready for a rematch?"

If Ray was, Ivy definitely was, and so they went again ... and again ... and again.

They each took a turn in the other's roller coaster, but they never gave up the front seats. And after the original tie they took turns winning, too, but they were all close calls and by the final ride Ivy had actually lost track of who had won more—which was distinctly unlike her and a sure sign that she had had enough. After the sixth or seventh trip she and Ray climbed out of their seats and staggered toward Dan.

"Ah, my little drunken sailors," he said in greeting. Ivy felt as if parts of herself—stomach, brains, backbone—were still back on the ride, draped over the turns and dips of the track. Dan slipped something from his pocket into the operator's hand, and they knocked fists together. It was a tip, Ivy knew. Dan was a big tipper, not a nickel 'n' dimer. The ride man saluted Ray and Ivy and said to come back anytime, ask for Sid.

Dan ushered Ivy and Ray over to a nearby bench and suggested they rest until they got their sea legs back. Ivy didn't know what sea legs were, but sitting on the bench waiting for them to come back felt just right to her.

"I signed us up for a tour of the town," Dan told them. If Ray and Ivy hadn't just roller-coastered their hearts out, they might have argued with him. They found tours boring. Educational. But right at that moment Ivy lacked the stamina—and the stomach—to put up much of a fight. Instead, when they had their sea legs, she and Ray followed Dan and dutifully boarded a waiting trolley bus and took their seats.

Ray sat by the window, since he was the smallest, and Ivy sat next to him, and Dan took two seats right behind them for himself. There were just a few other people on board—guests of the hotel, Ivy figured, not the general public.

"Now we can see for ourselves just what ole Hershey did with his fortune," Dan told them.

"What else is there to do with money but spend it?" Ivy asked. Her stomach had settled down a bit.

"Plenty!" Dan said. "Invest it. Save it. Launder it ... Ole Hershey was a philanthropist—gave his away, every last penny."

"He *did*?" Ivy frankly found it hard to believe. "People don't just *give away* fortunes."

"Blackstone did," Ray reminded her. "To us."

"After he died," Ivy said. She could understand giving away things *then*.

"Hershey didn't wait till he died. Gave as he got. Built a school, for one thing," Dan said.

"A *school*?" Ivy said. She was aghast.

"And a roller coaster," Ray piped up.

The tour guide asked for their attention then: the ride around Hershey was about to begin. A little microphone pinned to his lapel made his voice sound as if it were coming out of a radio, and as soon as he started to talk Ivy tuned in to her own thoughts. On the whole she found them more interesting than what most grownups had to say. She noticed, to her embarrassment, that Dan was taking notes, and wondered once again what had come over him. The place outside the bus went sailing by; every now and then, despite her daydreaming, a phrase or two of what Microphone Man had to say about it broke through.

Orphans, she thought she heard. *Orphans?* She listened up. *That* was who the school was for! Dan should have told her! Orphans interested Ivy. She considered herself something of an expert on the subject. She felt that she and Ray had come close to being orphans themselves during their time with Marietta and Lionel. Plus she had read plenty of books with orphans in them, and seen some movies. Now she stretched across Ray to see if she could spot any out the window, walking on the sidewalk. But she couldn't tell. They all looked like the general public to her. Microphone Man was talking about the school today and how things had changed, but Ivy tuned him back out and kept her eyes peeled.

Until she heard another word that got her attention: *jail.*

"*Where's* the jail?" she said. They were cruising down Chocolate Avenue and she didn't see any building that looked like a jail.

The tour guide stopped what he was saying, and repeated, apparently for her benefit, "Mr. Hershey believed that there would be no unhappiness in his town and therefore saw no need for a jail."

It took Ivy a second to register what he had said. When she did, it lifted her right out of her seat. "No *jail?*" she cried out. The people sitting across the aisle—an elderly couple, the woman's hair white as milk—tittered, but Ivy paid them no mind. "Did you say there's *no jail?*" she repeated. She spun around to face Dan. "No jail!" she exclaimed. "That's *great!*"

Dan gave her his slow and easy grin, nodded. But then he told her to simmer down and patted her hand. Ivy thought he was playing it way too cool. It seemed to her they had unearthed some important, potentially life-altering, information. She sat back down and the tour continued, but now Ivy was alert to everything, hungry to take in the streets and buildings and orphans and general public of Hershey, Pennsylvania.

"*Is* everyone?" Ray suddenly called out.

Once again the tour guide stopped what he was saying to address the question. "Is everyone what?"

"Happy?" Ray asked.

The tour guide smiled, and the couple tittered again, but no one gave Ray a real answer.

Utopias

Before they left Hershey, Dan let Ray and Ivy loose in the big mall of Chocolate World, among the stockpiles of candy and souvenirs for sale. "Thirty-three seconds," he told them, and set the timer on his watch. "Go." He'd buy them whatever they could gather in the given time; that was the deal. Ivy and Ray both went for the candy. Ivy put together a mixed bag, heavy on chocolate. Ray stuck with Good & Plenty and amassed bagfuls.

Back at the car, Dan announced it was time to get the Fitts family show on the road—Florida awaited them and Gladys wasn't getting any younger. Usually Dan preferred driving at night, but he said they needed to put in some extra hours. The normal rules applied:

no one could ask "Are we almost there?"; anyone could call for an ice cream stop; Ray and Ivy got final say on where they would spend the night.

Around seven o'clock the Treasure Inn Motel came into view. The sign in front advertised, in black letters, *Ahoy Mates, Kids Eat Free*. There was a big treasure chest mounted on top, with gold chains wrapped around it and daggers stuck in the sides. The vote to stay there was instantaneous and unanimous.

Ivy and Ray decided to swim before they ate for free, and after they swam, Ivy called a meeting in the baby pool, for privacy. Two grownups who wanted to swim boring laps had taken over the big pool anyway. Ray and Ivy had the entire little pool to themselves, and used the bumpy cement steps as their seats. Dan was stretched out on a lounge chair, asleep, *Writer's Digest* open across his chest.

Ray started the meeting with his same old question. "When do you think Carol will come?"

"When she's better," Ivy answered.

"I thought you said she was faking."

"Yeah," Ivy said, distracted. She was developing entirely new theories. "I think we're going to *move* to Hershey," she said.

Ray was balancing on his elbows in the water. Right away he entertained the possibility. "Roller coasters," he said appreciatively.

"Why else would he have brought us there?" Ivy asked.

"Roller coasters," Ray said again.

"No, Ray—think about it. There's no *jail*. No more going away. Why *not* move there? Plus we haven't moved in a long time," Ivy pointed out, and it was true. Before they landed at Marietta's big house, they'd usually moved every few months.

Ray shrugged, but not dismissively. He almost always gave Ivy the benefit of the doubt.

"*Or* ...," Ivy said—an even bigger idea was coming to her as the pool water lapped at her legs—"maybe he's after the fortune Gladys absconded so he can give it away. Just like ole Mr. Hershey-bar did."

"Give it away to who?" Ray asked.

"Orphans," she answered quickly. They were still on her mind. "Or the general public," she added, figuring that would surely cover it. The more she thought about Dan giving away a fortune, the more she warmed to the idea. It gave her a bit of a grand feeling inside. Also, the water in the pool was heated.

"Orphans?" Ray repeated.

"Didn't you *see* them?" Ivy asked. "They were all around us." In retrospect she was fairly sure that the kids she'd spotted from the bus *had* been. Orphans.

"Why?" Ray asked.

"Why what?"

"Why does he want to give his money to them?"

"So they'll be *happy*. Haven't you ever heard of *utopias*, Ray?" What Dan had told them in the car came flooding back to her. She felt deeply qualified to speak on the subject. "They're a real way to make your mark," she told him. "It's like making your own little world, exactly the way you want it to be. Just think of it—our very own town," she said. She stretched out in the shallow water. "What should we name our utopia? Fittstown?" she suggested. "Ivyville?"

Ray thought for a minute. "Shadow," he finally answered.

Ivy knew Shadow was the name Ray wanted to give a dog if they ever got one. "You can't name a town Shadow," she said.

"Why not?"

"Shadow or Shadowtown?" she said.

"Just Shadow," Ray answered.

"It doesn't even sound like a real town."

"It *isn't* real, is it—our own town?"

Ivy paused. "No," she admitted. "Not yet. But it could be."

"Will it make *Carol* happy?" Ray asked.

Ivy looked at him and didn't answer right away. Sometimes Carol was hard to please. "Maybe," she said.

They bobbed in the warm water, didn't speak. Ivy went back to thinking up names.

Then Ray asked, "Do you still think someone is after us?"

"*After* us?" Ivy repeated. It took her a second to remember what Ray was even referring to. Then she did a quick run-through of her usual suspects. The inky-haired waitress? No. Wolfie? No. Who was left?

"It's *Gladys* we have to keep our eyes on," Ivy decided. "She's the one who absconded."

They ate dinner in the motel restaurant and afterward played on the cracked shuffleboard court next to the pool. Then they pulled on their still-wet suits and swam again. This time Dan came in, too, and picked them up and tossed them around like footballs in the water.

"Can we call Carol?" Ray asked when they were finally back in the room. They had Room 224, on the second floor, close to the ice machine. Ray was staring at the phone on the nightstand next to the bed, as if Carol were already waiting on the other end to talk to them.

"Sure," Dan said. "Give her a ring, see how she's feeling."

A second later Ray laughed and said to Ivy, "It's Veddy. He said, 'Fitts residence'! Hey, Veddy, it's me, Ray." He was smiling and nodding, obviously happy to be connected. "We went to Chocolate World, on the roller coaster, is Carol there?" Just a moment later, he was excited all over again. "Hi, Carol, we rode the roller coaster ..."

Ivy lay on the big double bed and watched Ray talking to their mother, listened to his rush of news, all in a jumble, all of it tumbling headlong into his question at the end, "Are you better, can you come, when are you coming?" And then, on his end, silence. Ivy kept watching.

The news wasn't good; he wasn't hearing what he wanted to be hearing: that was easy to tell, even though—or maybe because—he didn't move or make a face. "Oh," he finally said, completely still, his voice smaller. And then, "Yeah, OK—here," and he held out the receiver to Ivy.

Ivy rolled over on the bed to take it. She was already a little mad at her mother for whatever she'd said to Ray that had made him sad. "Hi," she said—a flat, heavy word.

But Carol's voice sounded like music, all up and down and light and pretty, laughing in between the words.

"So you're still sick?" Ivy said. It wasn't really a question.

Then she heard what Ray had: that Carol was feeling better, but rather than try to catch up with them en route, she and Veddy planned to drive straight to Florida and meet them there. "Straight to the sunshine," Carol said.

Well, that wasn't so bad! At least she would be joining them! Eventually! Ivy glanced over at Ray again. He was pawing through one of his Good & Plenty bags. He looked OK.

"It's a plan!" Ivy said, and music started playing in her own voice again, especially as she started to tell about orphans and utopia. "It was real *educational*," she remembered to say.

A little bit later, Dan said he was going down to the lounge and left them to watch TV in the room.

"Stay outta trouble," they all said in unison as he stepped out the door and it closed behind him.

Ivy stretched out on the wide double bed. "Man, this is the life," she said. She mounded up the pillows around her. During a commercial she announced, "Dibs on mayor." She was thinking about their utopian town again, and who would run what.

"Mayor?"

"I could be mayor," she told him. "What do you want?"

"What else *is* there?" Ray asked.

"Get the notebook," she told him. "We'll make a list."

Ray dutifully retrieved the pad, and Ivy wrote down as many jobs and positions of power as they could think of.

When they were done Ivy read the list aloud. After

considerable thought, Ray chose dog officer, chef, and postmaster.

"General," Ivy added. "Postmaster *General.*"

Ray didn't say anything for a while, and when Ivy looked over at him she saw that his eyes were closed. "Are you asleep?" she asked. He didn't look like he was faking. With one last appreciative look around their hotel room, she snuggled down in the bed and decided to check out her own eyelids for pinholes.

Striking It Rich

Ivy felt it before she even opened her eyes—the thrum of the car on the road.

"Are we in Florida?" she asked, sitting up, looking around. Sunlight was streaming in.

"On our way," Dan answered. Ivy saw the beginning of a beard on his face. "One more place to check out, and after that it'll be a straight shot. Gladys isn't—"

"Getting any younger," Ivy chimed in. "So what's our last stop?" she asked.

"Another roller coaster?" Ray said. He had just woken up.

"Is it educational?" Ivy asked. She wanted to be warned.

"Absolutely," Dan answered.

Ivy's heart sank.

"Gems," Dan said. "You can never have too many rubies. Or know too much about them. Time to do some mining."

"Mining? For real?" Ivy immediately summoned up everything she knew on the subject. She pictured pickaxes and helmets with lights on them and climbing deep down underground with the seven dwarves. Why was there a canary flying around? Would there be a saloon to go to afterward, with swinging doors they could push apart and swagger through?

They were driving in the country again, over deeply rolling land, everything green, green, green. Wolfie's ticking car chugged up the winding, steep roads, and Dan told them to keep a lookout for arrows directing them to the Big Deposit Gem Mine.

They made a series of turns, followed the arrow at the general store, went up another hill to the entrance. From the parking lot, Ivy looked down a rickety wooden staircase to what she thought would be the mine—only it wasn't underground, and no one was carrying a pickaxe. Instead, Ivy saw a line of people

sitting on a wooden bench in front of a trough that
tilted down, pawing through mounds of dirt on their
screened trays. There was a little pond behind the
trough, its surface spotted with pink and white water
lilies, like expanded cupcake holders, and a few plastic
water jugs bobbing around. Over to the side stood a
hut with a porch; Ivy prayed it was a gift shop. As she
led the descent down the decrepit stairs, her flip-flops
clapping on each step, she already had her eyes peeled
for the glint and gleam of a giant ruby, even from up
above and far away. Ray was right behind her.

A large man with wild eyebrows who was planted

on a stool behind the hut's counter called to them as they approached, "Hey there, y'all in a hurry to strike it rich?" As soon as they got close enough he extended a beefy hand and introduced himself as Big Joe.

"Them ones over there—the rainbow buckets—are loaded," he told Dan, pointing to a batch of rusty containers filled with dirt. Ivy and Ray were eyeing what

the gift store had to offer, but Ivy wanted to hear what Big Joe had to say, too. "We load 'em with some semi-precious stones so the kids have something to find—keep 'em interested, you know. Them others"—and he pointed to another collection of buckets over by the pond—"they're pure."

Dan looked to Ivy. "What's your call?" he said.

Ivy didn't know what semiprecious meant, but she suspected that it wasn't as good as precious. And the idea of Big Joe putting stones into the dirt just so kids could find them sounded fishy to her, too—kind of like stacking a deck. She knew about stacked decks from Dan, and she knew enough to watch out for them. "We want the *real* dirt," she said, and she felt good saying so.

"Yeah," Ray seconded.

Big Joe reached out to take Dan's money. "Suit yourself. Go grab some buckets and Lacey'll get you started."

Dan told Ray and Ivy to help themselves.

"Aren't you coming?" Ivy asked.

"I'm going to pick Big Joe's brain for a while," Dan said. "You mine for rubies and I'll mine for information."

Downhill, Ivy thought—Dan had definitely gone downhill. How could information be better than rubies? Why talk when you could dig? Ray, though, was already over by the collection of buckets, looking into each one as if rubies might be sticking out of the top. Well, too bad for Dan; Ivy had her own lucky bucket to find. She ran over and started looking.

Ivy was hoping for some sort of sign about which one to pick—a surge or jolt from one of them as she passed by—but nothing happened. To tell the truth, they all looked like rusty buckets filled with clumpy dirt to her. Finally she and Ray just closed their eyes, spun around, and lifted up the ones they were pointing at when they stopped. They hauled the buckets over to the wooden bench and sat down.

A girl came over—the one Big Joe had called Lacey—and handed them each a screen-bottomed tray.

She had rings on seven of her ten fingers, and her breath smelled like cigarettes. Ivy figured she might be even twenty years old and found her both mysterious and beautiful. She showed Ray and Ivy how to dump clumps of dirt in their trays and hold them  down in the stream of chocolate-colored water running through the trough, to wash away everything but the gravel and stone. Dan was still up at the shed, leaning in close to Big Joe, as if he was already finding out every single thing there was to know.

"It's basically a process of elimination," Lacey told them. "Washing away everything you *don't* want, to get to what you're really after. And what you're on the lookout for is something with a slightly different color to it that feels a little heavier than all these other rocks and pebbles you pick up. And then, when you rub it against the screen, it doesn't break apart on you."

Ivy was eager to get started. She rubbed the gravel against the screen and watched the mud and silt flow off it, then drew up her tray and started sorting through. There was no sparkling ruby right off, nothing like the one in Dan's pocket, but she was hopeful.

"Is this?" she said, holding up one of the larger rocks. Lacey took it from her and rubbed it against the screen. It crumbled like a dry cookie.

"First life lesson," Lacey told her. "You think you got something and then it breaks."

Ivy was determined not to get caught with a crumbler again. A moment later she said, "How about this?" and held up another rock she had already rubbed hard. Lacey took one look and shook her head no. Ivy held up a number of stones for Lacey to inspect, but none of them was what they were looking for.

Finally Lacey told her, "Darlin', what you have in your tray is a whole lot of leaverright."

Ivy's heart momentarily soared.

"As in: leave 'r right there in your tray."

Ivy's heart dropped, and she had second thoughts

about not choosing the rainbow buckets. Maybe pure wasn't so great after all.

Meanwhile, Ray was silently, seriously picking through his pile, his little fingers carefully inspecting each pebble and stone.

Ivy emptied her tray and shoveled another handful from her bucket to inspect.

A loud, sunburned family had arrived and settled themselves next to Ivy and Ray on the long wooden bench. The father wore Bermuda shorts with knee socks. When he sat down, the board wobbled under them all. The kids, a boy and a girl, were bigger than Ivy but, she felt sure, younger. They had chosen rainbow buckets to sift through. And no sooner had they washed off the mud from their first clump than they started pulling out all sorts of colored stones. "*Lookit!*" the little girl called out every single time she found something. "Oh, Mama, lookit *this*!"

Ivy couldn't help herself: she always did—look—just to see what the girl was holding up. First it was "ochre," which Lacey told her the Indians used for war paint. The next stone, "picture jasper," looked to Ivy as if it had a black tree etched inside it. The girl unearthed flashy stones one after another from her bucket of dirt

and built up a mound of found treasure next to her. Ivy turned back to her own little pile on the screen—pure leaverright, she knew.

Next, Lookit's brother started in. "Lookit *mine*," he called out. His sister didn't, Ivy noticed, not even a glance, but Ivy did, and so did Lacey, and so did his mama, who exclaimed every time, "Oh, pumpkin, that's a *beauty*."

Ivy looked back to the shed, where Dan was still listening hard to Big Joe. Maybe he was striking it rich in the information department. But Ivy was beginning to doubt that she'd be so lucky in the gem department.

When Miss Lookit held up another stone for everyone to admire, a little *hmph* escaped out of Ivy. She leaned over to Ray and whispered, on the loud side, "They probably never even *heard* of a stacked deck."

Ray was so absorbed in looking through the mound of pebbles and rocks in his tray, rubbing them against the screen the way Lacey had showed them, that he didn't respond.

Ivy grabbed another clump of dirt from her bucket—she was almost down to the bottom—and slapped it onto the screen. She lowered the tray into the stream of water flowing down the trough, and the mud washed away and once again offered up its little mound of stones and pebbles for her to sort through. As she raised it back up, Ivy wanted more than anything to see a giant, glittering ruby waiting for her, but she braced herself for the probability that there wouldn't be one.

Suddenly Ray's voice rang out. "Is *this* something?" he said, holding up a rock the size of his thumb. Lacey walked over from the rainbow kids to take a look.

Ivy was already examining it herself, and she honestly didn't see why Ray was even asking. She could tell it wasn't anything—nothing at all like the ruby they were taking to Gladys, and not even beautiful. She shook her head and handed it back to him with a shrug, sorry about the disappointment he was in for.

"Lemme see," Lacey said, leaning over and taking the stone from him. She rubbed it hard against the side of the tray and held it up to the light. "I do believe you've got yourself something here. Let's go see what Big Joe says."

The next thing Ivy knew, Big Joe was ringing a bell and announcing on the loudspeaker that Ray Fitts had found himself a honker, a *super*-honker! Folks got up from the trough—including Mr. Bermuda Shorts and his whole Lookit family—and marched over to the shed to see for themselves and pat Ray on the back. Dan was beaming.

Ivy took another good look at what it was Ray had found. It *still* didn't look all that great to her, not even a distant relative of the perfect ruby Dan had discovered. It reminded her, in a funny way, of the mushrooms Wolfie had found in the woods, all dirty and rough compared with the ones she saw in the grocery store. Ivy stuck close to Ray, though, stood right next to him in the throng of people, and some of the pats aimed for him landed on her back, and she didn't mind.

After everyone had gone back down to the trough, all encouraged and energized that they'd be the next to strike it rich, Lacey came up to the hut and over to Ray and Ivy. "I'm on break," she told Big Joe. Then she held out her hand for another look at Ray's super-honker. "*Real* life lesson," she told him. "At the bottom of everything, somewhere, is that perfect gem, just waiting to be found."

Ivy liked Ray's life lesson a lot more than the one she'd gotten from Lacey.

"So what's the ruby *worth*?" Ivy asked of them all.

Dan gave her a grin and spread his hands. Ivy could

feel a "remains to be seen" coming. She turned to Big
Joe.

"Value's determined by the four C's," he told her,
and he bent back a stubby finger as he named each
one: "Clarity. Color. Carat weight. Cracks and flaws."
He nodded at Ray and his super-honker and said,
"You'll have to see how this one polishes up, decide
how you want to get it set."

Ivy knew what he was talking about. "Presentation," she said to Big Joe. "It's half the game."

"You said it," Big Joe agreed. "But your brother got himself a real gem there, a beauty."

Hard as it was not to have discovered it herself, Ivy was happy for Ray, no doubt about it, and glad to have a super-honker in the family.

By now the day was well on its way to hot. Ivy passed on Dan's offer to sift through another bucket, rainbow or pure. Looking and not finding—especially while everyone around her hit pay dirt—had taken a certain toll on Ivy. She was ready to have a cold soda out of the cooler and scour the gift shop for the best *it* had to offer.

As with most gift stores, the one at the Big Deposit Gem Mine did not disappoint. There were bags of polished stones, geodes, crystal necklaces, emu eggs. There were baskets of the picture jasper stones Miss Lookit had made such a fuss about, and each one held its own private hieroglyph. Ivy was especially drawn to one that looked like a spider, but that wasn't the item she eventually chose. Ray picked a little clock embedded in a chunk of granite. Ivy waited until the last possible moment—Dan was drumming his fingers—to make her decision. Finally she carried a little glass vial the size of her pinkie with a black screw top over to the counter. Dan paid and Ray leaned close to see what she had: the glass tube contained real gold flakes floating in a clear liquid. Ivy gave it a shake and made the gold specks rain down. "*Real* gold," she impressed on Ray, and a moment later, "Real *gold!*"

They said their goodbyes to Big Joe and Lacey, and then the three of them climbed the rickety stairs back up to the parking lot. It was satisfying, knowing that she and Ray were packing rubies and gold on their way out of the Big Deposit Gem Mine.

"Did you get what *you* wanted?" she asked Dan.

"You bet," he told her. "A wealth of information!"

Back in the car, Dan cranked up the air conditioner and told them to settle in for the long haul to Florida. He found a radio station that played songs full of twangy guitars and turned the volume up loud.

Ivy and Ray settled into their backseat cocoons and pulled out their treasures. Ivy shook her gold flakes. Ray rubbed his ruby over his shorts as if that could polish it up.

"What're you gonna do with it?" she asked.

Ray shrugged. "Give it to Carol," he said.

"*Really*?" What was it with some people, Ivy wondered, that made them want to give away their fortunes?

"Sure," Ray said. "She likes jewels. Remember when Dan gave her that diamond for Christmas?"

Ivy remembered perfectly. It was the only time she had ever seen Carol cry. And she remembered what Carol had said, that it was "from pure happiness." Ivy kept quiet for a moment and then told Ray, "You're a phi-lan-thro-pist," savoring each syllable and the chance to say so.

Ray shrugged his small shoulders. "Maybe it'll make her come sooner," he said.

Is That Right?

Florida was flat, and Ivy felt they'd been driving through it forever. She began to think they'd lived their entire lives in the car. Dan's face was stubbly with a beard. Ivy reached forward and swiped her hand across his chin. Sandpaper.

She turned back to look out the window. "Flat as a pancake," she said, looking out from the air-conditioned, sealed-in coolness of Wolfie's car.

"Flat as a potato pancake," Ray said.

Ivy had to disallow that. "Copying," she said.

Ray tried again. "Flat as a ceiling."

That was enough of *flat as*. Anyway, she was more interested in the signs she'd been seeing for a while now, the ones that said *Cougar Crossing*. She didn't actually understand what good the signs were—obviously *cougars* couldn't read them, so how were they supposed to know where to cross? But she had her eyes peeled for a jungle cat, in case. Ivy watched and watched—all that flatness made it easy to keep a lookout—but she didn't see anything except big black birds perched in the branches of the roadside trees, and a few, up ahead, pecking near the white lines of the highway.

"Vultures," Dan said.

Vultures! Ray made a silent, disgusted face. Ivy was already conjuring visions from old Westerns she'd watched with Dan on TV: blinding sun at high noon, birds circling overhead, just waiting to peck out the eyes of the thirsty, heat-crazed cowboys below.

"Feasting on roadkill," Dan told them. "It's their job. Garbage collectors get a bad rap."

Dan had a point, but Ivy preferred to consider the life-and-death scenario starting to take shape in her imagination. If Wolfie's car were to fail them now, or if they were to run out of gas and get stranded by the side of the road, how long could they possibly hope to survive? A minute? An hour? Four days? And who

would break the bad news to Carol? Poor Carol. She'd cry for *sure* then, like a river.

They were fast approaching the birds in the road. Ivy studied them gravely. Suddenly the vultures lifted their massive black bodies into the air, and Dan zoomed past. It was all over in a second, and Ivy felt that the birds had made a daring escape, saved themselves in the nick of time. A moment later she watched through the back window as they returned to their pecking places on the highway.

Their brush with death energized Ivy, and she faced forward again, eager to arrive. The distance to Everglades City had dwindled on the signs they'd passed, from 62 miles to 37 to 12 and now, finally, to 2. Ivy sensed that they were coming to the end of the road, heading straight to the edge of the map. A fine and delicious feeling surged in her, from deep in her traveling bones—the conviction that they were almost there, where they had set out to be, and that where they were was unknown and slightly dangerous. Ivy anticipated setting eyes on Gladys, who had absconded, and reminded herself not to miss a trick.

Finally, a sign with carved gold letters welcomed them to Everglades City. Ivy liked the name—she liked the *ever* in it—and mentally slipped it onto Ray's and her list of desirable destinations.

"We made it," Dan said as they sailed down the divided main drag. Things were quiet and seemed a little deserted, everything baking in end-of-day heat. Ivy noted an ice cream stand that looked like a little house, and read sign after sign promising the best soft-shell crabs and the best airboat tours, and lots of signs for real estate, too. She briefly wondered just what it was that made an estate real.

Now Dan was rounding a small rotary, steering the car with the bottom of his palm and his wrist—just the way Ivy loved to see him drive—past a fancy building with pillars, past a column of palm trees, grabbing the last turn off the circle, following the arrow marked *3 mile connector to Chockoloskee Island.* Ivy liked it that their final destination was an island—and that it, too, had a good name, one that made her think of gum, or some kind of dancing, or somebody laughing. She wondered if kids who lived there had to go to school. It struck her as the kind of place where maybe they didn't.

They passed by cabins for rent, and tiny houses, a trailer here and there, and then an old store with a single car parked in front of it—a long convertible with a picture of Elvis Presley painted on its spare-tire holder. Dan pulled in beside it and said he needed to wash up. "Make myself presentable," he told them, and Ivy remembered about presentation being half the game. Of *life*, she told herself, dramatically.

Dan went into the restroom to erase the beard off his face, and Ivy and Ray separated to search the store for the single best item to be found.

Ivy was checking out the candy selection when, only a minute later, Ray summoned her from an aisle over. When she rounded the corner, he shoved a perfect little alligator up to her face: tiny teeth and beady little eyes. It looked as if it had been coated in hard glue.

"Did you think it was real?" Ray asked. "Real dead," she answered. "But *was* it?" he asked, touching the gator's glassy eye with his finger. "Was it what?" "Real?"

Ivy didn't know if something could still be real if it was dead. That seemed like more than a fine distinction to her. "Oh, what *difference* does it make?" she said, as if she had far more important things to consider, and turned and picked up a plastic snow-globe filled with tiny palm trees and a flamingo.

Ray continued to study the baby gator hard. Finally he said, "It must be fake. No one would kill a real baby alligator."

Ivy had her suspicions, but she hoped Ray was right.

"Let's go!" Dan called. He was up at the counter,

checking out a local map. He was clean-shaven and smelled as though he'd slapped on some sort of cologne. Ivy thought his presentation was splendid. "Reunion time," he said as he ushered them outside through the wide, easy-swinging screen doors of the store.

Back on the road, theirs was the only car. The sun was a huge red ball, setting low. Scaly-trunked palm trees lined the road, and after a stretch, blue water sparkled on either side, and Ivy thought about diamonds and wondered if they were worth more than rubies. Ray kept asking when they'd see some *real* alligators. Sailing down the connector, shooting ahead toward the island—definitely on the straight and narrow, Ivy noted—she had the feeling that things were finally coming to a head.

"You gotta remember she's *old*," Dan said suddenly, and it took Ivy a moment to realize he was talking about Gladys.

"Older than Lionel?" Ray asked. Ivy and Ray's great-uncle Lionel *defined* ancient for them.

"Oh, yeah," Dan said. "And she's bound to be pretty frail at this point. She may be hard of hearing," he told them, "so speak up when you talk to her."

Somehow the little old lady Dan was describing didn't fit Ivy's picture of an absconder.

"She's probably just one step away from a nursing home," Dan finished.

Maybe, Ivy thought. And maybe not. She'd be on the lookout for disguises.

Once they were on the island, all the signs Ivy saw read *Dead End* or *No Outlet*. Little houses and trailers dotted the land, but no one was out and about. It looked a little bit like a ghost town—or ghost island—to Ivy.

At a street sign for Snook Alley, Dan took a quick left and slowed the car to a crawl. Little houses sat side by side on the right; the other side of the road was a dock, with small boats tucked into their moorings—a different kind of front yard from what Ivy was used to. Dan stopped the car in front of a raspberry-colored

shack
on stilts
set back just a
bit from the road.
"This is it," he said.
Ivy liked the looks of the
place right off. First of all, she
liked the stilts. She and Ray had been
given stilts for Christmas one year, and
they'd spent a lot of hours tripping each other
up on them. Ivy liked the color of the house, too—like
a drink that would taste good. She was thirsty.

They piled out of the car. Dan stared ahead at the house, ran his hand through his hair, and said, "Hope she's home."

"What?" Ivy said. "Why wouldn't she be?" After a moment's pause she added, "She's *expecting* us, isn't she?"

Dan's face looked a little pinched. "I thought we'd surprise her."

The plan sounded suspect to Ivy. "What if she's not here?" she said, but just then they heard a whistle from one of the docked boats on the other side of the street.

They turned to see a wiry, leathery-skinned woman standing in the back of a small skiff. Her fingers were still in her mouth from whistling. She removed them and called out, "Who're you looking for?" Her voice sounded as if it had gravel in it.

Dan answered smooth as silk. "How'd you know we are? Looking?"

She gave a little snort. "*Everyone* who shows up here is looking for something ... or looking to *hide*. Which is it for you?"

"Actually, we're looking for Gladys Mouton," Dan answered, and when she didn't say anything back, he added, "We're family."

"Is that right?" The brown, leathery woman nodded to herself. "Didn't know she had any."

"We're cousins," Dan said.

"Distant," Ray called out.

"Twice removed," Ivy added.

"Is that right?" the woman said again, bobbing in the back of her boat, looking them up and down. "Far as I'm concerned," she said, "you can't *get* far enough removed from family. Nothin' but trouble, in my book."

Who *was* this nut, Ivy wondered.

"So you're looking for old *Gladys*," the wiry woman repeated. "Well," she said finally, "she's not home."

Ray's and Ivy's shoulders slumped simultaneously. They were hot; they were thirsty. They didn't want to get back in the car.

"Is that right?" Dan said. Ivy thought he sounded pretty chipper. "Any idea when she'll return? Or where we might find her?"

The woman cocked her head. "A lot easier to get lost in these parts than it is to get found."

"I hear you," Dan responded.

No one said anything for a moment. Ivy swatted a mosquito on Ray's neck.

"Maybe you could help us," Dan said, "find our long-lost cousin."

"And why would I want to do that?" the woman said.

Dan grinned and held out his hands. "We've come a long way," he told her.

The woman didn't answer.

"We're family," he said.

She didn't move a muscle.

"We come bearing gifts," he said.

"Is that *right*?" she said, and she straightened her

taut little torso. "You shoulda said so in the first place!"
She hopped out of the boat and up onto the dock as if
she had springs in her feet. She raised her arm—thin
as a matchstick—and then brought it down in a quick,
sweeping bow. "I'm Glad Mouton, the one and only."

The Presentation

No sooner had Gladys admitted her true identity than she took off across the street. "Wouldn't dawdle if I were you," she called back to them. "Mosquitoes'll eat you alive."

Ray and Dan followed hot on her heels. Ivy resisted for a moment, endured one last bite, and then caught up to them in a hurry. As Gladys was passing by Wolfie's parked car she tapped its hood, then suddenly stopped and spun around. Dan, Ray, and Ivy piled into one another like a closed accordion.

"One thing I'd like to know," she said, speaking very close to Dan's face, "—just *why* was this car *ticking*?"

Ivy was all ears.

Dan didn't miss a beat. "Diesel," he told her. "It's a German model—louder engine."

"Not set to go *off*, is it?" she said, and Ivy was as offended by Gladys's insinuation as she was relieved to finally know the answer.

"No bomb," Dan assured her. He turned his palms upward. "Any other questions? Ask me anything," he offered, as if he actually welcomed Gladys's sneaking suspicions.

Ivy didn't. She found being on the other side of suspicion irksome. Besides, she had a question of her own. "Why did you say Gladys wasn't home when you were her the whole time?"

"A body can't be too careful," Gladys answered. "Specially when someone announces they're family. And I wasn't home—I was on my boat." She tapped again on Wolfie's car, then headed up the path to the raspberry house on stilts. She hopped onto a cinder-block step and up a few wobbly stairs. Gladys held open the screen door just long enough for the three of them to step onto the porch, and then let it shut so fast it smacked Ivy's bottom. Ivy counted the smack as one more indignity; she hadn't forgiven Gladys for tricking them.

Then, before one word was said, or long-lost-family kisses exchanged, Gladys snatched a bunch of tied-together palm fronds from the door handle and commenced swatting Dan with them.

Ambush—that's how Ivy saw it. Now they were being *ambushed*!

Gladys took a quick swipe across Dan's chest and then ordered him to turn around. Dan obeyed, and Ray and Ivy watched as Gladys flailed away at his back; the mosquitoes dotting his white shirt went flying. Finally she let the fronds drop to her side. She looked from Dan to Ray to Ivy and back to Dan. "So," she said, "we meet on the losers' porch," and then she let out a squawk—"Ha!"

"*Losers*!" Ivy repeated, incredulous. Glad was adding insult to injury!

"Where you *lose* all the mosquitoes you brought in with you," Gladys said, flashing for just a moment a brilliant white-toothed smile. Dentures, Ivy decided on the spot. Definitely fake. And as for her leathery skin, it reminded Ivy of the specimen Ray had found in the store: *alligator* hide.

"Here," Gladys said, handing over the fan of leaves to Ivy. "You two take care of yourselves. Kids know all about swatting each other."

Ivy grasped the leaves in her fist and for a moment didn't do a thing. They *hadn't* been ambushed, she realized. And now she had a chance to swat Ray. She made a quick mental adjustment and then, with a grand flourish, brought the leaves crashing down over

him, head to foot. She hopped around behind and did the same on his backside. When it was Ray's turn, he swung the leaves like a bat across Ivy's middle.

"OK there, slugger," Gladys said, and hung the leaves back on the door handle. She turned to face them and looked them up and down again, hard.

"Pleasure to finally meet you, Gladys," Dan said, and extended his beefy hand.

Gladys studied his hand but didn't take it. "Let's get one thing straight," she said, more gravel in her voice than ever. "Call me *Glad*. Being a Mouton's tough enough without having to frontload it with a name like Gladys."

"We'll call you *anything* you like," Dan told her. Ivy knew how obliging he could be when it came to changing names, but it seemed to her Dan was being *awfully* obliging to this sun-dried, ambushing trickster who wouldn't even take his hand. "Ivy and Ray," he continued, "allow me to introduce your cousin, *Glad*."

"Well, well, well," Glad said, "the whole famdamily. Whaddyaknow?"

"Actually," Dan said, "we're missing Carol, Ray and Ivy's mother. She was, ah, temporarily indisposed."

"Poisoned," Ray volunteered, but Ivy elbowed him.

Would he *ever* learn to play his cards close to his chest?

Glad's eyebrows shot up. "Is that right?"

"She's on her way now," Dan continued. "Due in sometime tomorrow."

"That right?" Glad said. "Anyone else I need to know about? People around here get nervous when strangers start showing up."

"Strangers!" Ivy objected. The description offended her—although, come to think of it, so did the notion of being related.

"Just Carol," Dan said. "And Veddy."

"The chauffeur," Ray volunteered.

Glad crossed her arms across her small chest. "Is that right? A chauffeur! Sounds like *some* branches of the family made out like bandits."

"Our Grampa Blackie pulled off the biggest heist—" Ray started in, and this time it was Dan who cut him off.

"I'm sure we *all* have lots of family stories to share. Plenty of time for that."

"But Gladys isn't getting any younger," Ray pointed out—as had been pointed out to him so many times.

Glad laughed a hoarse laugh. "Neither are any of

you," she added. Her smile flashed again, all those white teeth.

Ivy didn't have anything to compare it to, but was this how family reunions were *supposed* to go?

"Thirsty?" Glad asked. "Step inside and I'll give you something to drink. Then you can give *me* those gifts you came bearing ..."

Behind her back, Ivy made big eyes at Dan, but he smiled. He seemed to think everything was hunky-dory, going along just fine.

Reluctantly Ivy followed the others into Glad's house. It was a straight shot from the front door through to the back, as if the narrow, dim house were just a slight inter-ruption, with not all that much in between. Stepping inside, Ivy had the feeling that she was just as much on her way out again—and she didn't mind a bit.

Glad headed straight to an old refrigerator in the corner, a big, heavy contraption. She yanked open its door, which looked to Ivy like it probably weighed five hundred pounds, and told them to grab themselves something cold.

The ancient cooler was stacked with small brown bottles. The ones in front weren't labeled, but in the back Ivy spied some root beer and grabbed two bottles

for herself and Ray, their hourglass shapes thrillingly frigid in her hand. Glad handed Dan one of the brown bottles and took another for herself.

"Is *that* the nursing home?" Ray asked. He had gone over to the window and was looking out at the small white house just a stone's throw from Gladys's.

Glad's eyebrows shot up. "That's Pete's place," Glad told him. "He runs a number of businesses out of that house, but I don't believe one of them is a nursing home."

"Oh," Ray said. "Dan said you were just a step away from one."

Gladys whooped. "Oh he *did*, did he?"

Dan coughed a little on what he had just swallowed. "Great place you got here," he said.

"Can't beat a shotgun shack," Glad said. "Especially when it's all you got." She took a swig from her bottle.

Ray and Ivy exchanged looks. "Shotgun?" Ray said.

"Don't have one," Glad apologized. "Anymore. But if some fool ever gets it in his head to fire on this place, the bullet'll pass through the front door and out the back clean as a whistle, won't disturb a thing. Won't even rustle a feather."

Glad *had* feathers—Ivy had spotted them almost first thing—a bucketful, close to where Ray and Ivy were standing, ten times bigger and brighter than the feather Ivy had found at the restaurant. The comparison panged her, and she itched to snatch one out of the bucket and twirl it between her fingers.

"Si'down," Glad told them. "Take a load off."

Ivy and Ray plunked down on the floor, beneath the window, and Dan said he was glad to stand for a while, after such a long ride.

"Suit yourself," Glad said, and trotted over to the back of the room. She started digging around in a pile of stuff. When she straightened up a moment later she was holding two big hooks and a chunk of heavy chains. "For you," she announced.

Ivy froze as Glad quick-stepped toward Ray and her, toting the chains and hooks. Images of dungeons instantly pulsed inside Ivy's head: shackles and only crusts of bread and gruel for food, thirty lashes, and Ray so old he had a three-foot beard. But Glad moved right past Ivy and Ray to the other end of the room, where she hung a hook and chain from one of the silver rings mounted on the wall.

"Grab yourself a bed," she ordered, pointing to a

pile of netting next to the old refrigerator. She crossed
to the opposite wall and linked another hook there.

Ray immediately descended on the pile and a
minute later was dragging a hammock over to Glad.
She attached one end to the chain, and Ray linked
the other. Suddenly, before them: an innocent white
hammock, suspended between the walls of the room,
inviting as could be, and not a bit like a dungeon.

Ivy quickly squatted down over the heap of netting. She hadn't *really* been fooled, she told herself. But what kind of relative greeted family with hooks and chains? She banished the images that had started to play inside her head, extricated another hammock from the pile, and brought it over to Glad and Ray.

"I'll get that," Dan said, coming over to attach it to the higher rings in the wall. That was when Ivy realized just how small Glad was. She was one of those short people who loomed large. Dan had the second hammock suspended just a moment later, and rocking net bunk beds suddenly beckoned to Ivy and Ray.

"As long as you're here, you'll need a place to sleep," Glad said. "This is as good as it gets." She turned to Dan. "You take the couch on the losers' porch." She plopped down on what appeared to be an old car seat and said, "Now—about those gifts you mentioned ..."

This wasn't how Ivy had pictured it happening—the reunion, Glad's warm welcome, the presentation of the Mouton family heirloom to their oldest living relative. But Glad clearly wasn't one to dawdle. "Show me what you got," she said, and held out her hand.

Dan glanced over at Ray and Ivy, eyebrows raised. They stepped in closer to witness the moment. Dan

cleared his throat and produced the Mouton family ruby in Wolfie's special box. "A token of our affection," he began, "seeing as how we're family and all ..."

"Don't rub it in," she warned, and she took the box, lifted it next to her ear, and gave it a little shake. Then she held it out a distance in front of her and squinted at the family crest, stamped in gold. Finally she gave a low, rattle-like chuckle.

Ivy felt the urge to say something impressive. "The language in the ribbon," she told Glad, "is Latin."

"Something about nuts," Ray offered. "In the family."

"Well, you got *that* right," Glad said.

Ivy stole a look at Dan. She couldn't tell how the presentation was going. She wanted to help. "It's stamped in genuine gold—" she said.

"Foil," Ray finished.

Glad looked up at both of them. "Is that right?" she said, flashing that sliver of a smile again. She lifted back the top, and there sat the sparkling red jewel, nestled in velvet padding. "Ha!" she squawked. She plucked the jewel out of the box and bounced it in the palm of her hand. "Long time since I laid my eyes on one of *these*." She looked up at Dan and her eyes narrowed. Then, quick as a wink she had the ruby back in its box, snapped shut, and pocketed away. She made it disappear almost as fast as Dan did!

Was that *it*? Ivy asked herself. No *Thank you*, no *You shouldn't have*, no tears of pure happiness? She acted like she *deserved* the jewel!

And now Glad was telling Dan, "You can help me smoke my mullets"—as if he hadn't just given her a family fortune. "Later I'll take you all on a tour of paradise. You two," she said, addressing Ray and Ivy, "do what you want." It sounded like an order.

Dan gave them a thumbs-up and followed Glad out back. Ivy did an imitation of Glad's springy walk for Ray's benefit, but it was lost on him—all he had eyes for were the suspended hammocks in front of them. Clearly he was itching to hop in and swing. Ivy had her doubts about settling in at Glad's, but the hammocks *were* inviting, no two ways about it. And if Ray was close to pouncing, then it seemed to Ivy she ought to pounce herself, and make sure to claim the top one. She took a running leap. Ray did too, and a second later they were both swaying, arms and legs spread. Ivy had to admit it: she liked the accommodations. A lot more than she liked Glad.

"Do you think Carol will get here tonight?" Ray asked from below.

"Maybe," Ivy answered. And it wouldn't take her long to find out Dan had given Glad the ruby. So much for smooth sailing on the way home.

"What're mullets?" Ray asked next.

"What?"

"Mullets."

Ivy didn't know. "Things you smoke," she said.

"Like cigars?"

"Kind of," Ivy said, and then, in case she was wrong, "But not exactly."

They didn't talk for a while, just rocked. Their hammocks were in sync. Ivy found the swaying conducive to thinking.

"Are we in paradise?" Ray called up to her, clearly ready to believe.

"No," Ivy answered, definitively. The hammocks were nice but not heavenly. Ivy was pretty sure they weren't even in utopia. "That's just what she called it. You can call something anything you want, but that doesn't mean it's what it is."

"Oh," Ray said. Ivy could picture his mouth, a little round *o*.

"It's like Wolfie calling his house a castle," she told him. "It doesn't mean it really is. Or that we're really in paradise."

"But we *could* be," he said, just the way Ivy sometimes did.

"Remains to be seen," she answered. "Anyway, we have to be on the lookout. Glad could *abscond* again." The word still carried a certain thrill. "Plus she's so suspicious of everything!"

"I like Glad," Ray said.

"You like everyone," Ivy reminded him. Would he never learn?

"I don't like Marietta," he said, defending himself. Marietta had been really mean when Ray wet the bed. "Glad's better than Marietta."

"*Any*body's better than Marietta," Ivy pointed out.

"Glad is family," Ray said. He rocked the hammock faster. "She's thicker than water."

"You're just copying Dan," Ivy said, as if *she* never did. "You don't even know what that means. Plus she doesn't even *want* to be—family. Remember what she said about you can't get far enough removed?"

Now that Ivy thought about it, she was offended all over again. It was one thing not to much want Glad, but quite another for her not to want them. How *dare* Glad not be glad to be related!

ALLIGATORS IN PARADISE

"All right, you two, let's get outta here," Glad called to Ray and Ivy. "The fish are smoking and your father's threatening me with family history."

They leaned out of their hammocks and dropped to the floor. When they reached the porch, Dan and Glad were already outside and Glad was marching across the street on her matchstick legs. She led them to the dock and down to the boat she'd been in when they first saw her: a beat-up flat-bottomed skiff. Its outboard motor appeared to Ivy to be mostly duct tape and wire.

Ray and Ivy squished in on either side of Dan on the plank seat, and Glad positioned herself in the back. "You *start*," she commanded the bandaged old engine,

and then gave a series of rapid-fire pulls on the cord.
The engine coughed and sputtered as if the last thing
on earth it wanted to do was start, but then it did, just
as Glad had ordered it to. She fiddled with some levers
until she had it purring nice and smooth, and then she
maneuvered them away from the dock, out onto open

water. The breeze felt good and blew everybody's hair back off their faces.

"Are we going to paradise?" Ray asked.

Ivy rolled her eyes. He'd never learn.

"You're already there," Glad told him. "I'm taking you somewhere I can hear myself think."

Ivy liked the sound of *that,* at least. Hearing herself think was one of Ivy's favorite things to do.

Within minutes Glad had them deep in the Everglades, weaving through touching towers of mangroves—"walking trees," she called them—maneuvering in and out of little inlets, a labyrinth of water and land. The air was thick and the growth around them teeming with life. Insects set Ivy's neck on fire.

"No-see-ums," Glad said, and gave her arm a good smack.

"Remains to be see-um," Ivy whispered to Dan.

"Normally we'd be eaten alive," Glad told them, "being out this time of day. But the Gulf wind has blown most of the bugs inland."

Ivy felt another bite and swatted her thigh. The bugs that had stayed obviously liked her best. She leaned into Dan. Scrunched beside him, Ivy was able to believe that she and Ray weren't being kidnapped, but she *did* harbor worries about getting deeply, hopelessly lost. Ivy remembered what Glad had said about it being a whole lot easier to get lost in the Glades than it was to get found, and it seemed to her they were puttering their way farther and farther into a million-piece puzzle. Or no, not a puzzle, a jungle—*that* was where they were, Ivy concluded—surrounded by hanging vines and branches, dinosaur-like birds landing in their giant-sized nests. Plus it was starting to get dark. And even though it was getting late, it seemed to Ivy that everything around them, the entire outside world, was awake—and watching them. Deeper and farther into a foreign world of unclear boundaries between water and land Glad puttered along, clearly in her element.

She led them into an especially overgrown mangrove tunnel, dark and creepy—filled, Ivy suspected, with creeping things. Ivy couldn't see how they'd ever manage to turn around and get back out. Glad pushed on. Finally, just when Ivy was certain there was no end to the tunnel, they emerged into a beautiful, peaceful, otherworldly lagoon.

And there, in the middle of a still circle of water, Glad killed the engine.

Everything went suddenly quiet—or so Ivy thought until she really listened. Then she heard a cacophony of sounds all around her. The sounds of the jungle, she thought: plunks in the water, as if fish were jumping up or frogs were jumping in, and beyond that, rustlings and stirrings in the deep underbrush. Now and then, from up above, a snap, a swoosh, a lone, exotic call. She squished even closer to Dan and Ray on the plank.

Deepening dusk made everything shadowy and blurred, but moonlight lit the water and drenched the lagoon in which they sat. Ivy could still make out Glad's wiry frame and sharp edges. Now she saw occasional glints around the edges of the lagoon. She had a fleeting memory of the diamonds sparkling on the Gulf when they had driven across on the connector to the island, but that had been in sunlight and suddenly seemed long ago. They were in a different place now, different from any place Ivy had ever been before. And these glints weren't diamonds. They were red, like rubies!

"So," Glad said, her voice sandpaper on the night, "welcome to the sweetest place on earth."

Ivy was still staring out at the water, transfixed by the gleaming red sparkles—floating, gliding, moving together. Pairs of them. Coming closer. Suddenly everything inside of Ivy seized up. "Alligators!" she choked out, her mouth as dry as crumpled paper.

Glad chuckled. "*Course* they're gators," she said. "What did you think those red eyes were? Priceless *jewels*? Ha!" Her squawk reverberated across the water.

Ivy held her breath.

"Alligators?" Ray repeated. He sounded positively thrilled.

Ivy leaned as far into Dan as she could lean. Now she only *stole* glances at the floating jewels. The last thing she wanted was eye contact.

"Nothing like being surrounded by a bunch of gators to help you think straight," Glad said. "Gets you right down to the heart of the matter. And speaking of that—we have our own matters to discuss, don't we?

Family matters. I'd wager there's more to your visit than meets the eye. So now that we're all reunited—and here, among friends—how about you tell me the *real* reason for your visit." She paused. "What're you after?"

Deeply distracted though Ivy was by the ring of alligators, Glad's question still managed to register on her. It sounded so familiar! It was *her* question!

"Glad," Dan said, as if he'd been cut to the quick, "trust me!"

"Oh, I trust you all right," she said. "About as far as I could *throw* you."

Ivy gasped. It was only too clear where Dan would land if Glad threw him. Ivy scanned the perimeter of floating red eyes. She imagined the teeth that followed. It was more than she could bear. "How *dare* you not trust us!" she cried out. "When all we did was come and give you a great big ruby! Worth a *fortune*!" she threw in, for emphasis.

"Fortune!" Glad squawked. "*This?*" In a flash she had pulled the box from her pocket and flicked back the lid. She held it at arm's length and the moonlight danced across the ruby's facets.

Even though she was up to her eyeballs in alligators, Ivy once again marveled at its beauty.

"I know exactly what this thing is worth, and let me tell you—it ain't much!" Glad said. She snapped the box shut with a ferocious little click—like a mouthful of teeth closing. Then Ivy heard a loud plunk in the water. Her heart skipped. Had Glad tossed the ruby overboard? Would Ivy have to dive after it? She skimmed the surface of the water for ripples, a bubble, some mark of where it had gone. All she saw were rubies ... eyes ... alligators—surrounding them!

Next to her Dan shifted in his seat. Was he about to go after it?

What about Ray? Would *he*?

If Ray did, Ivy was definitely going after him, no doubt about it. She saw it all in a flash—the fight for her brother's life, yanking him free from the alligator's jaws. She would do it; she would! Then she heard him speak, her brother: "So the ruby's *fake*?" he said.

Ivy turned her attention back to Glad. The jewel box was still in her hand.

"Wolfie said it was gen-u-ine," Ray said.

Ivy called off her life-or-death battle with the alligator.

"Right," Gladys agreed. "A genuine synthetic."

"Synthetic?" Ivy repeated. She didn't know the word, didn't trust it.

"Man-made," Glad said. "As opposed to dug out of the earth."

"Unearthed!" Ray said.

"Not this baby," she told them. "This one got grown in a laboratory. A *replica* of the real thing, but no more real than that mumbo-jumbo stamped on the box."

"Hey," Dan said, "that's the official Mouton family crest you're talking about!" He didn't sound offended, though. He sounded amused.

All of which left Ivy genuinely confused.

"Oh, I know all a*bout* that family crest," Glad told them. "I was there when Blackstone drew it. Copied it out of a book, threw in a fancy-sounding motto in Latin—like anyone with half a brain would give two hoots for that nonsense! Ha!"

Ivy felt a little squeamish.

"So now that we got *that* straightened out," Glad said, "why don't you tell me what you're up to, what you're *really* after?"

Ivy listened to herself think and didn't hear one clear answer.

"Family!" Dan cheered. "Blood's thicker than water," he pointed out.

Ivy wished he hadn't—she saw *no* need to talk about blood. And water. Not now.

"Mmmm," Glad said. "So love of family drove you here? To deliver me this little piece of eye candy? Oh, yes indeedy," she continued. "An act of generosity, pure and simple ..." She paused. "And you expect me to *buy* that? Do I *look* like I was born yesterday?"

"No!" Ray answered loud and clear. "Dan says you're *really* old."

Glad's squawk erupted across the lagoon. "Ha! Is that right?" She nodded toward Ray. "Well, at least you got one straight shooter in the bunch!"

Ivy took umbrage at not being included. "Some people *do* give away valuable things," she informed Glad. "Phi-lan-thro-pists," she said, syllable by careful syllable.

"Mr. Hershey did," Ray contributed. "Roller coasters."

"That so?" Glad said. "Well, what I want to know," she continued, leaning in toward Dan, "is what you planned to get in return."

It was jungle quiet for just a moment, and then Dan spoke. "All right," he said. "I'll come clean."

Come clean? Ivy forgot about the alligators.

"I had an ulterior motive for making this trip and giving you the ruby."

"*Now* we're getting somewhere," Glad said.

Was Dan going to reveal his plan to create a utopia? Or explain how making a fortune ran in the family? Or maybe accuse Glad of absconding? Despite a cascade of possible theories, Ivy didn't know *what* to expect.

"I'm writing a book," he said.

Oh, come *on*! Ivy thought. Surely he could come up with something better than that!

"You *are*?" Ray said.

"Based on our family," Dan continued.

"Crackpots and criminals," Glad declared. "There's your title."

Why was Dan sticking with such a lame story? It might have worked at the gates of the amusement park, but now they were surrounded by alligators. And Glad wasn't born yesterday!

He wouldn't drop it, though. "I've done a lot of research, but you can get only so far with the official version of things. I need other versions, the story behind the story—that's what I'm after. You may be my last best shot at the truth."

"I *am* a good shot," Glad concurred, her voice a bit of a purr.

"But I wasn't sure you'd cooperate. I knew from the research that you and Blackstone didn't exactly part on good terms."

"That stinker," Glad spat out.

Now Ivy was really confused. "*You're* the one who absconded," she blurted.

"Is that *right*?" Glad said, narrowing her eyes and leaning in toward Ivy as if she were going to take a bite. "Says *who*?" She didn't wait for an answer. "Sounds to me like somebody sold you a bill of goods. Led you down the primrose path. Pulled the wool over your eyes. Bam*boozled* you."

Had Ivy been *had*? But she'd *read* it! With her own eyes! In black and white! She felt a little woozy.

"That's why we need your side of the story," Dan said. "Otherwise Blackstone's version will be the only one. He'll have the last laugh. Don't let an old family feud stop you from setting the record straight. I brought the ruby as a peace offering."

"You mean you brought that synthetic bauble as a bribe—so I'd spill the beans and you could take it to the bank," Glad said. "You *knew* that ruby wasn't real, didn't you?" She widened her stride in the back of the boat.

It seemed to Ivy that the eyes on the water had multiplied and were circling even closer.

Dan exhaled. "I cannot tell a lie," he said. "I knew. When I first came across it I had my doubts. And Wolfie knew what was what, and then Big Joe confirmed it, too."

"So you were trying to pull a fast one on me!" Glad sounded triumphant.

"Not at all," Dan protested. "All part of my research. It's important to know how reliable your source is. I needed to know how much *you* knew, and if you'd call a spade a spade."

"So you were testing me," Glad said.

"You could say that," Dan admitted.

"Didn't trust me," Glad said.

Dan shrugged. "About as far as I could throw you."

Glad let out another squawk. "You may be all right, after all."

"Of *course* we're all right," Ivy said. How *dare* Glad still doubt them?

"Any relative of Blackstone is suspect in my book," Glad replied.

Oh, no, Ivy thought. *Another* book?

"We can't help it that Blackstone was our relative," Ray piped up. "Just because we're related doesn't mean that *we're* stinkers," he added.

Glad didn't answer right away. Then she flashed a quick grin—all those bright little teeth of hers. "So you're telling me I should give you the benefit of the doubt, is that right?" She knotted her thin arms across her chest. "You know I could leave you here with the gators for dinner, don't you? *Their* dinner." She gave a little snap of her own mouthful of teeth. "But this one—Ray—he's a good one. I like you, boy. So whaddyasay we wend our way back home and cook up those mullets? Then we'll see if you're up to hearing some *real* family history." With that, she crouched down a bit and started yanking the cord to the engine. "Don't even *think* about not starting," she commanded, and on the very next pull it caught.

In an instant she had them motoring out of the lagoon, into the long, deep tunnel of mangroves, their passage witnessed by a lakeful of gleaming red eyes.

The Real Story

Things were different after their interlude in the lagoon. The heat of the day had dissolved into the darkness. The bugs had stopped biting. Now that Dan had put all his cards on the table, she could relax, Glad said.

"The cat's out of the bag," Dan agreed.

"More like the *book*'s out of the bag," Ivy said. She was still getting used to the idea. She would never have said so to Dan, but compared to the reasons *she*'d dreamed up for their visit, writing a book struck her as, well, a little boring.

"Will we be in it?" Ray was asking. He obviously liked Dan's plan. "Will there be pictures?"

Ivy hadn't thought of that. Portraits, perhaps. She

turned her head to the side and imagined a classic profile. "Will you use our real names?" she asked. The thought of *IVY FITTS* in print pleased her.

"I'm considering a blend of fact and fiction. That seems to sell best these days," he told them. "I may need to change a name or two to protect the innocent."

"In *our* family? There *aren't* any!" Glad squawked. She gunned the engine then, and they picked up some speed across the open water.

Cooled by the breeze, zipping along, Ivy took heart. Writing a book wasn't the *worst* thing in the world. Especially if Dan threw in a near-death encounter with the alligators, and Ivy's daring rescue of Ray.

"I don't know about any of you," Glad called out over the noise of the engine, "but I'm starving." She speeded up even more.

As soon as they got back to the shack, Glad fried up the mullets and served them sizzling hot out of the pan.

"What *are* mullets?" Ray asked again, after he'd cleaned his plate.

"Best fish in the world," Glad told him. "Even if they don't get much respect. Mullets have it rough—they

get chased by everything." She finished off her last bite. "My kind of fish," she said.

Ivy suspected it was close to midnight by the time they had the dishes cleared and were settled back on the porch. But no one said anything about going to bed—or even to hammock. Instead, Glad fetched some more home brew for herself and Dan and more root beer for Ray and Ivy. It was as if they'd landed in some other world, Ivy thought, where all the rules evaporated—or no, as if there weren't any rules to begin with. Maybe it *was* paradise after all.

Glad brought the kerosene lantern over and placed it in the center of the table. She fished in her pocket and produced the ruby in its box, set it down in front of them. "So," she said. "Are you ready for the *real* story?"

Dan flashed his million-dollar smile, and Ray and Ivy both nodded. For the first time ever, family history was going to keep her awake instead of put her to sleep.

"Oh, that Blackstone Mouton," Glad began. "He was one dirty bird."

Ivy thought it was a strong beginning, so much better than Blackstone's blah-blah-blah about *illustrious and accomplished ancestors*.

Glad took another swig of her brew. "As big a crook as there ever was."

"What about Grampa Blackie?" Ray said. "*He* pulled off the biggest heist in California history."

"That's *nothin'*," Glad said. "I'm talkin' about the robber baron himself. Blackie robbed banks, but Mouton robbed everything—the land, other businesses, his workers, his own family. He'd do anything to make a buck. Only difference between him and Blackie is that Blackstone mostly got rewarded for what he did, and Blackie got caught."

Ivy thought it was a *fine* distinction. Having been

caught herself a number of times, she harbored a deep resentment toward those who got away with murder.

"Anyway, what happened happened a long time ago. Before I believed I'd ever get old." She looked at Dan and Ray and Ivy. "Before any of you were even born," she added.

Ivy was skeptical about things—especially important things—that supposedly happened before she was born. That there even *was* a time before she was born was hard for her to imagine. She gave Glad the benefit of the doubt, though. She wanted to hear the story.

"Blackstone was looking for a get-rich-quick scheme he could make a killing on. His first venture had gone bust. That's when he heard about these newfangled rubies being made over in France. Decided to import them and sell 'em over here. But he was short on cash. That's where I come in. He sweet-talked me out of my hard-earned money to buy the first stash." She leaned in toward Ray and Ivy and wagged a finger in their faces. "Never go into business with a relative," she told them.

"That's what Blackstone says in *The Last Laugh*!" Ivy said.

"Doesn't surprise me one bit," Glad responded.

"Any man who'd steal my money wouldn't think twice about stealing my words and calling 'em his own. The dirty bird."

"Plagiarist," Dan said, and Ivy liked the word although she didn't know if it was the name of a bird or a description of Blackstone.

"So I forked over my dollars and he bought a bag of

synthetic rubies and sold 'em like hotcakes to fat cats in New York City."

"Cats?" Ray said. "Fat?"

"Rich people."

"Oh," Ray said.

"Did he tell them the rubies weren't real?" Ivy asked.

"Ha!" Glad squawked. "What do you think? He put 'em in fancy containers and used words like *perfect* and *flawless* and *crème de la crème* to describe them. Drew up that family crest for some instant history. Never said they were real—but never said they weren't, either. There are lots of ways to tell a lie, and Blackstone tried all of them."

"So *that's* how the first family fortune was made," Dan said.

Glad clamped her teeth shut with a quick little snap. "Don't talk to me about fortunes," she said. "I was one of the *less* fortunate—never laid eyes on one red cent. Blackstone plowed everything he made on the rubies into his other schemes, then tried to pay me off with baubles and promises. By then I was disgusted with the whole shebang. I took off and never looked back, and the rest, as they say, is history. He went on to make a *real* fortune. And how did he do it? Steel!" She let out another squawk.

Everyone was quiet, then. Glad took a sip of her home brew, then set the bottle down as if the story she'd been telling was over. But it didn't *feel* like the end to Ivy. It was so unfair! "So you didn't get *anything*?" she cried. Even the scent of injustice incensed her.

"Oh, I made out all right," Glad said with a chuckle. "Got *exactly* what I wanted, matter of fact." She pushed back her chair and went into the other room. Ivy, Ray, and Dan sat in the soft glow of the lantern, listened to bugs fling themselves against the screens as if they were desperate to join the family meeting.

A moment later Glad was back, toting the bucket full of feathers. "I got the *real* beauties!"

"*Feathers*?" Ivy and Ray said in unison.

Dan just listened.

"I was always partial

to them," Glad said. She smoothed them with her crooked fingers. "Plus they were a sweet reminder of Blackstone's first failed business. He sold egret feathers to hat makers in the city, shipped 'em by the ton from here in the Everglades. Made a killing on them, too—until the demand for feathers dried up. Once he couldn't make a buck on them he said they were useless—except as a centerpiece for his fancy old dining room table."

"Oh" was all Ivy managed to say.

"What *are* they worth?" Ray asked.

"Far as I'm concerned," Glad said, "they're price-less."

Ivy had a sudden memory of what she had told Ray back at the Close-to-Home Restaurant: that feathers had to be worth something. "I knew it," she called out, just for the record.

"Not that I'd ever sell 'em," Glad continued. "Stolen property, you know—those poor egrets were *robbed*. Not to mention killed. Poached!"

"Eggs?" Ray asked.

"Birds," Glad clarified. "Poachers shot 'em and plucked 'em and when the government sent out rangers to stop the poachers, the poachers shot the rangers, too. All so Blackstone could get his feathers and fancy ladies could get their hats. It's a wonder there are any birds at all left down here—and that's only because fashion changed. Ladies started wearing felt hats, and that was that for Blackstone's operation. He moved on to rubies, and finally to steel. I figured this last batch of feathers belonged with someone who'd at least appreciate them." She plucked a particularly dazzling specimen from the bucket and slotted it behind her ear.

Ivy studied Glad in the soft light of the kerosene lantern. How beautiful the feather looked against her alligator skin.

Dan tapped Wolfie's fancy box, resting on the table. "So this little item isn't worth a great deal to you after all," he said.

"That bauble's not worth a thing," Glad answered him. "To *me*! But it's all relative—some people would die to have one." She reached over and pushed the box across the table toward Dan. "Maybe you should give it to someone who'd genuinely appreciate it."

Dan's eyebrows shot up. "You sure about that?" he asked.

"Sure as shootin'," Glad said. "I prefer the real thing."

"Well, that's awfully generous of you, Glad," he told her.

"And to tell you the truth, I think
Carol'd be tickled pink to own it."

It was a wonderful thought: Dan giving Carol the
ruby, Carol wearing it on her finger. She might even
cry again, Ivy thought: from pure happiness.

"Look," Ray said suddenly, and he produced *his* ruby,
his super-honker—not as quick as Dan and Glad could
pull things out, but with a certain grace.

Glad zeroed right in on it. Ray handed it over and
she examined it closely, then let out a deep cluck of
approval. "Now *that*'s the real McCoy," she declared.

"How can you tell?" Ivy asked. "So quick?" It still

rankled her that she hadn't been able to spot one herself.

"Easy," Glad answered, bouncing Ray's super-honker in her hand. "First of all, it has some weight to it. More important, it's not perfect. Look at that flashy one in the box and you'll see there's not a flaw in it." She leaned in toward Ivy. "Nothing *real* comes without a flaw."

Ivy and Glad looked at each other without blinking, as if they were having a staring contest. Finally Ivy turned her attention to Ray. "Life lesson number three," she told him.

"Where'd you get it?" Glad asked.

"I unearthed it," Ray told her. "At the mine."

"Good work," Glad said.

"You can have it." Ray gave a little shrug.

Glad startled. "Is that right?" she asked him, and Ivy thought she heard just a sliver of suspicion in Glad's voice.

"Give him the benefit of the doubt," Ivy advised. "He means it."

"Sure," Ray told Glad. "I was going to give it to Carol, but you gave her yours, so you can have mine. Plus you like the real thing."

Ivy watched Glad watch Ray. Glad cleared her throat with a little growl and finally told him, "Well. That's downright ... generous."

"Runs in the family," Dan said. And then he broke into a chorus of "Mele Kalikimaka" and everyone joined right in. Glad and Ivy even added a little harmony at the end.

Finally Glad smacked her hands on the table and declared they'd had more than enough of family matters for one day. "Time to turn in."

They all stood up from the table. Ivy had a momentary desire to squirt out the kerosene light, but she decided not to reveal that particular family tradition. She suspected Glad might use a real gun.

Whole Famdamily Reunion

Ivy slept a deep, delicious sleep that night, swinging in the hammock strung across Glad's shotgun shack. She was awakened from it by Ray's foot against her back, rocking her. "Do you think Carol will come today?" he asked, first thing.

She had barely opened her eyes, but she felt the answer in her bones. "Yes," Ivy answered him.

"Do you think she'll like it here?"

Ivy pictured Dan handing over the ruby to her. "Yes," she said again, and Ray gave her another push with his foot. Ivy drifted back toward sleep.

"Do you think Carol knows Dan's writing a book?"

Ivy sighed. What was it with all the questions? She'd

gone to sleep last night convinced she finally had all the answers. "I doubt it," she told Ray. Dan played his cards close to his chest.

"Do you still think we're moving to Hershey?" Ray asked.

That theory seemed long ago and far away. "Probably not," she answered.

"How about building a town of our own?" he continued.

Ivy swayed. She was loath to give up her utopian dream, even though it was pretty clear they wouldn't be getting a fortune from Glad to finance it with. "Dan could make a killing on his book," she said. She'd begun to see its potential as a runaway bestseller.

"Or the movie," Ray said.

Ivy flashed back on the whole episode at the amusement park—Dan sweet-talking the lady about the book, the movie, scouting on location—and felt a pang for ever having doubted Dan's story. "A major motion picture," she declared now. She could practically taste the popcorn. "We might still get our own town after all," she said.

"Shadow," Ray insisted, for its name. He kept rocking Ivy's hammock with his foot.

The more Ivy thought about it, the more she realized how right they'd been about practically everything— the pursuit of family fortunes, the value of feathers, dentures. She considered starting a brand-new list—of all the things they'd gotten right—and was just about to have Ray fetch their notebook when they heard a car pull up. She and Ray were out of their hammocks in a flash.

As soon as they hit the porch they spotted the limo—almost as long as Snook Alley, gleaming in the sun. And there was Ivy's feather, still tucked in place next to the hoodie.

Dan was already outside and down the path. Ray lunged for the door to follow, but Ivy grabbed him back. "Watch," she told him. She had a sudden, sure feeling about how this particular reunion needed to go.

Dan threw open the limo door and reached inside to offer Carol a hand. Ivy held her breath as Carol stepped out into the sunshine, blinking in the light as if a million flashbulbs were going off around her. Her dress was checkered, red and white, and her sandals were open-toed and her toenails were bright red. Ivy took it all in like a vision. Dan wrapped his arms around Carol and lifted her off her feet in a swirl.

Suddenly Glad appeared behind Ray and Ivy on the porch. "Not *another* reunion," she said. "You people don't know when to quit," and she disappeared back into the house.

Now Dan was escorting Carol up the path to the porch—like a queen, Ivy thought. They stepped through the door and Ray threw his arms around his mother.

Ivy felt suddenly quite shy and didn't know *what* to do. She grabbed the palm fronds and started swatting them all. But after only a few swats she dropped the brush and joined in the family knot.

When they finally untangled themselves, Ray urged Dan, "Give her the present."

Dan couldn't have been more obliging. Suddenly,

instantly, there it was, the ruby, pinched between his fingers.

The color rose in Carol's cheeks. Her hand flew up to her chest. "For *me*?" she said.

"Nobody but you," Dan answered.

It was like they were singing to each other, Ivy thought.

Carol teared up and her eyes got all shiny and looked more beautiful than ever.

"I don't know what to say," she said.

"Then don't say anything." Glad had suddenly

reappeared on the porch—with an exquisite orchid tucked behind her ear.

"Allow me to introduce our long-lost distant relative, Glad," Dan said.

"Pleasure, I'm sure, Gladys," Carol said, extending her hand.

"Glad," Ivy corrected. "A fine distinction."

"These kids of yours are all right," Glad said, taking Carol's hand. "It's a mystery to me how they landed in our sorry family."

A strange urge had been building in Ivy since she'd first spotted the limo, and it suddenly overtook her. "I'll be right back," she said, and she sprang out the door and down the path. With a "Hiya" to Veddy and one quick swipe, she had the feather out of the hoodie and in her hand and was headed back to the house. Glad held the door and let it smack her bottom when it closed.

"For you," Ivy said, turning around to Glad and holding out the small, spotted specimen. What had come over her, she wondered. She was giving away her treasure!

Glad's eyes narrowed. "Is that right?" she said. Then she smiled and her teeth shone. Ivy had no doubt they were real.

"Ivy," Carol cooed, "how generous of you."

"Glad told us some great stories," Dan told Carol. "She's a gold mine of information, a real gem."

Glad swatted the compliment away. "It's all relative," she told him.

Later that day, while Glad and Carol and Dan sat out on the porch with home brew and root beers, Ray and Ivy

convened a meeting in the upper hammock. Ivy opened the notebook right off.

"New list?" Ray asked.

"Whole new thing," she told him, turning to a blank page.

"What?" Ray asked.

"Oh, Ray," she said. "Haven't you ever heard of a *book*?" It was so obvious to her that they needed to write one.

"About what?" Ray asked.

"What *really* happened on our summer vacation," she said. "It's up to us," she told her listening, willing brother. "Otherwise we'll get stuck with the official version."

"Won't writing a whole book take a long time?" Ray said.

Ivy agreed it would. But, she promised him, "It'll be worth it."